To Jessica from
Grandpa and Grandma
Grote

W9-BHY-351

TREASURE IN THE ATTIC

TREASURE IN THE ATTIC

by

Elizabeth J. St. Maur

A Geneva Book

Carlton Press, Inc.   New York, N.Y.

©1985 by Elizabeth J. St. Maur
ALL RIGHTS RESERVED
Manufactured in the United States of America
ISBN 0-8062-2229-8

TREASURE IN THE ATTIC

I

"Say, fellas, know anything about that old trunk in the middle of the attic floor?" Beth knocked on the door of her brothers' room.

"Advance and identify yourself," came Tom's authoritative voice.

"Well, I can't advance until you open up, and I don't know who you want me to be today," explained Beth. Then she added, "I don't even know who you are today."

"We're Feline Defenders of the Future, and we require complete computerized identification. Here." A slip of paper was shoved into the hall from under the door. Beth read aloud in a clear, distinct tone, "Elizabeth Rachel Baker, 24 Silver Maple Lane, Shady Oaks, New Jersey, U.S.A., North America, Western Hemisphere, Earth, Solar System, Milky Way Galaxy, Universe."

The door swung open. Beth advanced.

The Feline Defenders of the Future sat cross-legged in a semi-circle and smiled up at their sister. For a minute she wondered how they'd opened the door without getting up. Then she saw the end of the rope on Dick's wrist. It ran through a pulley mounted horizontally on the wall inches above the floor, then hooked to the base of the door. The hook made it detachable.

"Very clever, Dick," the girl admitted. "But what about the trunk?"

"We found it earlier today when we were up there looking for something else. It was so far back under the eaves we'd never noticed it before. We shoved it into the middle of the floor until we could get Pops to open it for us," Tom explained.

Beth was about to say maybe he wouldn't open it, when she remembered how seldom Pops refused. He was so proud of them. She had even been annoyed lately, and ashamed of the feeling at the same time, that her brothers were named Tom, Dick, and Harry. She was being teased by some of the students from Ashwood who were attending Shady Oaks Junior High for the first time this fall.

Her brothers were so well known in their own town that Mom seldom had to explain their names anymore. Beth remembered hearing her tell Mrs. Benson next door, "Tom went slightly silly when the doctor told him he had three sons. We were just delighted with our baby girl, and named her after me. So, of course, the first boy would be Tom, Junior. When Beth was two, we began praying for a son. Dr. Burhmann did tell us to expect more than one, but as long as one was a boy, it would be the answer to our prayers. Well, as I said, Tom was so pleased he said the first thing that came into his head. The people at the hospital had the names on the records before we could change them. I had a grandfather named Richard, so we let that stand. We'd never had a Harry, but he just seemed to follow naturally."

And Harry had followed naturally ever since. Beth looked affectionately at her brothers. Tom was the leader. He had always been. Long before he organized their original club, Tom's Cats, in the first grade, he had been the spokesman for all three. Dick was the scientific one who managed to figure out a way to do the fantastic things Tom thought up. Harry just naturally followed. Harry wasn't as tall as his brothers, but he moved as quickly and even more gaily and rhythmically. He was more alert to the music and general beauty of the world, and he had insisted on calling himself Rusty as soon as he could talk.

Realizing she hadn't spent much time with them since she'd been going to junior high, Beth squatted down to complete their circle. "So what's this about defending the future?" she asked companionably.

"The future is where we will be living, you know," began Dick.

"And, now that we're growing up, Tom's Cats, and even the Jungle Kings, are kind of baby names for us," continued Tom.

"So, we thought we'd absorb the sixth grade science project on ecology into our lives, change our club name, and blow Mr. Lenkowski's mind on Monday with all the ideas we gave him for the Academic Fair," finished Rusty.

"You can't do much about the world's ecology on a rainy Saturday afternoon, can you?" asked Beth. She herself had a cold and wasn't even allowed over to listen to records with Susie Benson. Deciding she might as well follow Mom's suggestion and dig out her winter clothes from the attic, she'd gone up right after lunch. That was how she saw the trunk, and her curiosity had brought her down to the boys without even a woolen mitten to show for her trip.

"We were up in the attic this morning to see how much insulation there was. We thought we could offer to rake up leaves, earn money for insulation, and get it up before the first snowfall. That way we'd be helping the family and working on the project, too. Saving energy, you know. Also, our slogan is ECOLOGY BEGINS AT HOME. We won't worry about the world until maybe next week," Tom grinned.

Pops was used to the boys doing that sort of thing. Uncle Bud Benson and his son Dan had their own construction company, and the boys had been gofers for Bud and Dan since they could walk. Whenever work was needed on the Baker home, Bud was consulted. Pops, the accountant, sat down with Bud at income tax time each year, and was available for emergencies at any time.

The two families had a good working relationship. The youngest Benson, Josephine, called herself Joey and spent as much time in Bess Baker's kitchen as in her own. Beth and Susie were best friends, and played endlessly in the Benson's cellar game room. Joey's December birthday put her a grade behind the boys, but this made her a little sister to them. Dan, gorgeous, handsome Dan, was everyone's favorite. He was a freshman at a midwest college now, and not expected home until Thanksgiving. Both moms were in daily contact, by phone if not otherwise.

Although Dan was older, he had always had a reasonable amount of time for the triplets. They'd made him an honorary king of the Jungle Kings a couple of years ago. Tom was a panther, Dick a leopard, and Rusty a jaguar. Dan? Yes, a lion. The family said it was pretty awful, and the boys themselves almost changed it when people began teasing them about their great biblical knowledge. Dan, however, assured them it was just what he'd have chosen if it had been up to him. After all, lions were kings of the jungle, weren't they?

"We're looking for some new ecology ideas," continued Dick. "The collecting of bottles and cans for recycling and cleaning up parks and school playgrounds is still important, but they're old stuff. We want something supernew."

"I was pushing the idea that BEGINNING AT HOME could be as close as your own mind. That would give different things for our list for Mr. Len. We could study the water cycle. We could take a class trip to the Pine Barrens to see first-hand the damage last summer's fires did," Rusty added.

All four began generating ideas.

"Word games: crossword puzzles, find the hidden word, how many three or more letter words are in p-h-o-t-o-s-y-n-t-h-e-s-i-s...."

"Art: posters of the food cycle; before and after of river scenes...."

"Shoebox dioramas...."

"Sure! We Feline Defenders will write a list of ideas that will top all the lists handed in on Monday!"

The four laughed at each other and applauded their own wisdom. They each took a piece of paper and jotted down ideas. They decided to work as individuals, and when no one's pencil had moved for three minutes, they combined the four idea lists into one.

Happy in each others' company, they pulled out a deck of cards and began to play. Beth felt no need to be Miss Teen of Maple Lane just then. She was comforably at ease with her brothers. There were times when they annoyed her, and she them. They argued and shouted, but no more frequently than did most brothers and sisters. She'd never been one of Tom's Cats or the Jungle Kings. There was something about her more like a soft cuddly kitten. Her dark hair shone, and her large gray eyes smiled warmly at the world.

After an hour or so, Tom glanced out of the window to find the rain had stopped and there were patches of blue in the autumn sky. He suggested they try to salvage some of the day. So, panther, leopard, jaguar, and cuddly kitten unwrapped their legs, broke the friendly circle, and went their separate ways.

The boys decided to take a football and ride over to the school in hopes of finding a touch game in progress in the yard there. If not, they could start practicing a few passes and maybe some of the fellows would come along.

Beth determined to head for the attic and make that search for the warm clothes. She pulled down the steps, mounted resolutely, and once again stopped short as she saw the old trunk in the middle of the floor.

II

"Mom, know anything about that old trunk in the middle of the attic floor?" Beth boosted herself up on one of the kitchen stools.

Without looking up from the potato she was peeling, Bess smiled. "There you are, Beth. Are you feeling better? When was the last time you took an aspirin? Did you get to the attic for your winter things?" Mom was a dear, thought Beth, but she did often carry on conversations without listening to her talking partner. But then, so did most adults, Beth had noticed. Parents were the worst offenders. The Bensons were sort of the exceptions that proved the rule. Susie and Joey sometimes just sat and talked with them! And, now that she thought of it, Dan paid more attention to the younger children than most college men did.

"Well, dear, did you?"

"Did I what, Mom?"

"Did you get upstairs to look for your winter things?" Beth was a dear, Mom told herself, but heedless. Someone once said that children don't listen carefully to their parents because they know the parents will repeat until they get an answer.

"Yes, Mom. I brought down all my stuff. Some won't fit, I guess, but I'll go through them all later. What I wondered was: Whose is the old trunk in the middle of the attic floor?"

"I didn't know there was anything in the middle of the floor up there. I try to keep the center clear, so we can at least walk around. I wonder how it got there?"

"The boys said they found it far back under the eaves and pulled it out so Pops could open it," explained Beth. "None of us has ever seen it before, though, and I wondered if you knew anything about it."

"Beth, you're sniffling again, and your voice still sounds scratchy. Please take some more medicine and lie down until supper. Maybe I shouldn't have sent you up to the attic today. It may have been too chilly."

Beth knew better than to continue about the trunk now. Mom

11

was too distracted, getting the meal and worrying about her only daughter's possible cold. It was difficult being a delicate child. Beth was always the first in the family to get a cold. Then after everyone had had it, she got it again on the way out. She missed a lot of school and a lot of fun. Not just being unable to go to outdoor activities, but things like not being cheerleader because the skirt was too short to be warm enough. Thank goodness her voice was good; she'd made the glee club.

As she climbed the stairs to her room, the phone in the hall was ringing. Pops had gotten a long cord on this extension so that whoever wanted to carry it to a room for privacy could do so.

Beth picked up the phone and started walking as she spoke into the mouthpiece, "Bakers. Beth speaking." She was sure it was Susie, but gave the formal hello her parents wanted, just in case.

"Hey! You sound pretty good! I thought you had a cold. Wasn't that why you had to stay in today?"

Assured that it was Susie, Beth kept the phone in her hand while she stretched out on the bed. Mom had said to lie down. "Oh, I sneezed once or twice, and you know how Mom worries about me. Then when she saw it was raining, I was automatically grounded," Beth explained. "But I found the most interesting looking old trunk in our attic! Actually, it was the boys who found it...."

Susie interrupted, "Sounds great, but I called to ask if you could come over tomorrow. You can tell me about the trunk then. See, I got to the mall today and bought Lanky Luke's new record. There is a poster that comes with it, and a six-page booklet of pictures of him at his concert in Atlantic City!"

Beth, hearing her brothers come upstairs, remembered it would soon be time to eat. She hadn't taken her medicine yet. "Sue, that's terrific! Listen, how about if I call you back in a couple of hours? Or, maybe you could come over here after supper?"

"I have to stay home with Joey tonight. The folks are going out. But call. We can talk as long as we want and Joey can watch the TV she wants."

"OK. 'Bye." Beth hung up, took her medicine and once again stretched on the bed. This time she pulled a blanket over herself. The boys were moving about across the hall. When they had first begun being interested in cats, Pops had taken advantage

12

of that interest to point out that a principal characteristic of cats was their being able to move about very quietly. The three were usually together, so their presence was rarely undetected, but they made less general noise than most boys Beth knew. They didn't pretend to be tricked by Pops, he'd simply given them more than one good reason for doing what everyone wanted.

When the Bakers first moved into their house, the second floor had a rather standard plan. The central hall had a bathroom at one end. Two rooms of equal size opened out on each side of the hall. Pops and Mom took the front bedroom on the left, with windows opening on the east and south. Beth's room was also on the left, giving her the southwest. The boys were put into the front room on the right, and the other was a sort of upstairs playroom catchall.

The boys soon became cramped and, in fact, Pops looked in one day and couldn't find them! Actually, each was flat on his stomach under his bed in some sort of game. That did it, though. Pops went over to Bud that very evening.

That was at least five years ago, but Beth remembered the pleasant weeks after Christmas that winter. Bud came the first night to check stresses and structure and that sort of thing. It was decided to knock out the wall dividing the two rooms on the right of the hall, automatically doubling the boys' space. Although this was on the north side of the house, there were east and west windows, too. Tom's Cats soon assigned themselves definite lookout positions for a 180-degree watch around the Baker home.

A sink was installed on the part of the wall that formed the hall bathroom, taking advantage of the plumbing casing already there. The door opposite Beth's room was widened. Bud had suggested the sink to lighten the traffic of six people in one upstairs bathroom. It was also convenient for all the reasons growing children need water.

It was Dan, already in junior high and as good a carpenter as his dad, who suggested the widened doorway. Dan was also the one who came into Beth's room and nailed up shelves all along one wall. She had lost her place in the playroom, and was wondering what to do with her dolls, books, and stuffed animals. He admitted having done the same thing for his sisters at Susie's request. So it was really Susie's idea, but Dan was kind enough to take the time. Beth would never have had the courage to ask

13

him herself.

That January marked the beginning of the closeness of the two families. It was the first year Susie and Beth were in the same homeroom at school and had the same homework. Beth was repeating third grade. She had missed two months the winter before with pneumonia.

When Bud and Dan went to the Bakers' after supper to work each night, Susie came along. She helped Beth move out of the playroom, and then just naturally stayed to talk and play.

Joey hadn't started school yet, but Mrs. Benson said she wasn't going to stay home and miss all the fun. Mom and Joy Benson stayed downstairs and talked and exchanged needlework skills. Mom showed her neighbor how to do macrame and needlepoint, and then learned how to knit and crochet. The Bensons became Uncle Bud and Aunt Joy to Beth and the boys; Dan and his sisters acquired an Aunt Bess and Uncle Tom.

Joey spent most of the time with Beth's stuffed animals and usually fell asleep before everyone gathered in the kitchen for a snack. She was annoyed the next day when she found she'd missed it, but mumbled and grumbled terribly when they tried to wake her. They usually just let her sleep on the sofa and travel home across the yard in Bud's strong arms. Since she had no school, she slept late the next morning.

Speaking of sleeping, Beth must have dozed off herself. Here was Pops, gently shaking her shoulder. "Feel like coming down to eat, Princess?" he asked. "Mother said you could have a tray up here if you want. Take a warm bath, get under the covers, and we'll give you chicken soup room service on request."

Beth sat up and then stood to give her father a loving bear hug. "No, Pops. I'm OK. Thanks." They walked down the hall together, arms still around each other. It was then that Beth remembered about the trunk in the attic, but she decided to let the boys ask about it. It was their find.

III

"So, Beth, did you get to see what was in the trunk in your attic?" The girls had gone to their favorite seats in the cafeteria, and Susie had just set her tray down and swung her legs over the bench.

"Not yet," answered her friend with a sigh. "Yesterday we went to Aunt Alice's for a surprise party for Grandma's sixtieth birthday. Our family parties are usually fun, and I think Grandma was actually surprised. It was the second best way I know of to spend a rainy Sunday."

Susie's blue eyes twinkled as she laughed sympathetically at her friend. "The best way being, 'Listening to the rain patter on the attic roof while you sit before an open trunk, searching through all the things stored and forgotten by long dead ancestors.'"

"Why, my dear, you've been reading books!"

"Yes, every once in a while. Seriously, though, finding anything valuable in an old trunk only happens to people in books. You know, discovering a valuable coin collection or a deed to an oil well or gold mine. What does happen to the Beths and Susies in Shady Oaks Junior High is the Hallowe'en Dance in the gym next week."

Both girls thought about this while they ate their hot dogs and sipped their Cokes. Then Susie spoke again, "One good point about being on the committee for a Hallowe'en anything is that you can begin whenever you want. No fussing about a theme. We do have a super surprise, though. Something that has actually never been done at a Hallowe'en at S.O.J.H.!"

Beth was all attention. "We're overdue for new ideas, that's for sure. But you will keep the outdoor stuff, won't you? And the costume prizes? Mom came up with just the right thing for me to be both warm and disguised." Beth was anxious not to lose the traditional activities.

Susie reassured her, "We'd no more omit costume prizes than Miss Kinnet could do away with the grade school children's parade around the block. Every adult in town would have her head. They line up along the streets for it. The old ladies who have no children in Elm Street School find something in the stores along the route they need right away. Mothers with babies go for a walk in the brisk autumn air, and the police simply must be there to see that everyone's OK."

"Of course," agreed Beth. "Joey was over explaining to us last night, as if we all didn't know. They have class in the morning and when they go back to school after lunch, they go in costume. They line up as usual when the bell rings, but instead of going

15

right into school, they parade around the block. The parade ends in the auditorium, where each class takes a turn going on stage and the principal, PTA president, and class mother give prizes for funniest, prettiest and all the other kinds. Then they go to their classrooms, being sure not to sit in their own seats. Each teacher then tries to guess her own students. Then they sit with their friends, eat, clean up, and go home. The best part is knowing that on Saturday they'll get dressed up again for the town celebration at the firehouse." Beth was looking a bit wistful.

"You're just a kid at heart, aren't you?" smiled Susie, who was often surprised to hear herself poking fun at Beth. She had done so only a few minutes before, teasing about the rain on the attic roof. Beth knew it was not done unkindly; she sensed that Susie was in a hurry to grow up and trying to shed the things she considered childish.

"Tell me about the costume that will keep you warm and be a good disguise," Susie asked.

"I thought you'd never ask!"

"I didn't think I had to, really, but I'll even coax, if you want," answered Susie, playing along.

"We probably won't have time for coaxing; the bell should ring soon. So..."

Beth's words were drowned by the loud ringing of the bell sending them back to class. They parted, agreeing to meet at the Baker house that night for homework and costume planning. Susie would see Beth's and they'd work on an idea for one for her.

As she climbed the stairs to her room at home after school that day, Beth was conscious of someone else being upstairs, too. Pops was at work, Mom in the kitchen, and the boys had outdoor practice of some kind, she thought. Still, she sensed a presence. A troubled one. Was Susie right? Could she be reading and romanticizing too much? Had the Hallowe'en spirit gotten such a strong hold on her that she imagined sad ghosts in her own upstairs hall?

Suddenly she laughed aloud. An unmistakably human sound had broken the silence. Ghosts don't sneeze! The door to her brothers' room was ajar, so she pushed it open. There was Rusty, sitting on the window seat. His head and one arm were pulled through his football jersey, while he absent-mindedly blew his nose.

"Hi, Sis, c'mon in," he invited.

16

Beth laughed again. "You gave me quite a scare, Rusty."

"Boy, you sure scare easily these days, if a sneeze can spook you. I didn't know ghosts sneezed, though. That would be rough, if they could catch colds. Living in damp cemeteries and being chilly all the time."

"You really are a great guy. You even have sympathy for ghosts!" Beth loved her whole family, but Rusty was the one she found easiest to talk to. They were good friends. No one else had gone along so easily with Harry's wanting to call himself Rusty. No one else spent so much time playing cards and generally entertaining Beth when she couldn't go outside. Another sneeze made Beth ask, "What's up? I thought you fellows had a special practice today. Are you catching cold?"

Rusty explained, "I don't think so. I forgot my suit, came home for it, and had to go to the attic for my shoes. Stuff's been moved around up there, and I kicked up some dust looking for them. I must have some in my nose. I've been sneezing ever since."

"Is the trunk still there?"

"Why wouldn't it be?"

"I don't know. Just that Mom may have moved it to straighten up. You said stuff was moved."

"Trunk's there." Rusty looked at the cleated football shoes he'd brought down. "These don't fit anymore and, you know, I'm surprised to find I'm glad. I was just sitting here thinking when you came up. Tom and Dick are good guys, and we have fun together. But lately I have the feeling that there is something else I'd rather do than be with them all the time. I'm not sure what it is, and it bothers me. It may be my drawing. Until I'm sure, I can't explain why I don't want to always join them. And while I keep being with them, I haven't the time to think it out."

Beth recalled the troubled presence she'd felt earlier. "That is tricky," she agreed. "Maybe it will help if I tell you we all know you are a bit different. An OK different, of course. We never all sat down and had a great meeting or heavy discussion or anything like that. We just sort of knew when buying presents for Christmas or birthdays that you'd prefer, say, a paint set to the mechanical stuff Tom and Dick liked. You're the only one who chose a nickname, too."

"You mean, if I sometimes say, 'No thanks,' to them, they won't mind?"

"They'll probably mind, but they won't be surprised, I think," answered Beth.

"Thanks, Sis!" exclaimed Rusty, shedding the football gear. "I'm going to ride over to the field right now. Since these shoes don't fit, I can't play. I'll tell them and then just sort of drift around on my bike and think. It's a great October afternoon to be outside."

Beth took advantage of his distraction to give her brother a quick hug, and left him stepping into his chunky brown shoes and tugging on his favorite pullover. Her eleven-year-old brothers did not look favorably on hugs from a teenage sister.

Beth crossed the hall and dropped her books on her bed. She heard Rusty dash down the stairs and slam the door, exiting into his great October afternoon. Then she turned into the hall again, pulled down the steps to the attic, and began climbing, telling herself, "I'll just stick my head up and check on the trunk."

IV

"Trunk! Trunk! Trunk! What's with you, Sis, you know something we don't?" Dick took her by surprise, so she shouted back.

"I don't know anything except what you boys told me! Maybe YOU know something and don't want me asking questions!"

Tom's head surfaced through the stairwell. "You two at it again?"

"She keeps asking..."

"He won't listen..."

Beth and Dick were standing in the attic next to the trunk. Usually, on Saturday mornings, the children were sent upstairs after breakfast to give their rooms a general straightening and clean-up. At least, that's what they were supposed to do. This day, when Dick got to the hall, he found the stairs down, so he climbed them. Minutes later, Tom heard the noise and climbed, too.

Dick turned to his brother. Beth let him talk. He could be louder anyhow, when he tried. She knew Tom wouldn't hear her above Dick.

"I came up here for our warm jackets and found the Dark Haired Mystery Lady fiddling around with the lock here. Pops

18

said he'd open it. Why is she messing around?" Dick sounded really upset. "It's like the thing is alive and haunts her! Pretty annoying."

Tom turned to the Mystery Lady. "You do seem to take a special interest in this trunk. Mom's upset, too. I heard her talking to Pops last night about how you keep asking about it. Do you know something we don't?"

"Honestly, Tom. I'm just curious. Pops said he'd open it. True. But he forgets what's not right in front of him. Since it's OK by him if the trunk is opened, I just thought I'd give it a try.

"Mom may come up someday and shove it back. You know how she hates things to be out of place. Then it will be harder to get to."

Dick assured her, "Mom won't shove it. It takes at least two to move that. We had a hard time, didn't we, Tom?" Dick had a shorter temper, but it cooled fast. Also, he enjoyed any problem that could be considered scientifically. Suddenly he was Archimedes' only living rival.

"She wants it opened, not moved, pal," Tom reminded him. "How did you make out with the lock, Sis?"

Beth was still provoked, "I didn't really get to try. Chief Inspector Nosey Baker here, calling me names and quizzing me why I'm in my own attic and what I know and...what business is it of his, anyhow?" She stopped. Both boys were looking at her. They had bent to check the lock more closely, but the unfamiliar, strident tone in her voice made them turn toward her. She and Dick sparked each other more than any other combination of family members, but the fuss seldom lasted even this long. There was no sulking or days of not speaking.

The silence of the boys now made Beth listen to her own voice. She, too, was surprised at its tone. She said, softly, "Sorry, guys."

"This lock is too rusty to open," Dick told her. "We'll work on it later. Have to get some rust remover. We could always break it. But if we can clean it up and save it, that would be better."

Tom added, "Sure. We'll get to it later, since we have Pops' permission."

Beth, remembering that they not only had Pops' permission, but they also had Pops' habit of 'getting to it later,' was not very much encouraged.

She helped the boys find their warm jackets and watched them

19

climb down the steps. Then she just stood, thinking about her recent anger. She had been close to tears. Such a stupid thing to be so mad about. For a while she had almost hated Dick! Maybe she felt a bit guilty about trying the lock. But he had been mean to call her all those names, making fun of her. She had a right to be there, and to try opening the trunk, didn't she?

She thought of the films they showed at school about growing up. Sudden anger and crying and worrying were part of it, they said. If boys felt those things, too, this family was in for some terrific times!

That may be why Dick had jumped on her, saying her curiosity was annoying. A year ago he, too, would have been curious and automatically helped her with the lock.

And Rusty was questioning himself and others more lately. He was spending less time with his brothers since their talk the other afternoon, she noticed. Or did she notice more since their talk the other afternoon?

Come to think of it, she had also had mixed feelings about Susie this past week. When they got together Monday night and Beth showed her friend the costume she and Mom had nearly finished, Susie exclaimed delightedly. Then she suggested that she heself get one just like it only with the colors reversed. That would confuse the judges about their identity, and help win the prize for hardest to guess. Susie also figured a way to hide their hair.

Later Beth began to think that Susie had more or less stolen her idea. She told herself this was silly. Susie hadn't asked her to make the second costume or, for that matter, to do anything extra. There were a couple of other girls who'd be only too glad to have Susie as a partner. Also, Susie'd shared the secret of the surprise with her. The rest of the committee wanted no one but themselves to know they had a real gypsy fortune teller for the evening.

Instead of the traditional spooky Hallowe'en decorations, they were using a Good Fortune theme. Silver circles had been cut from the aluminum foil so useful in kitchens, and were being hung, along with the familiar crepe paper streamers and skeletons and ghosts, to represent Coins of Fortune. The prizes were wrapped as treasure chests, and in one corner of the gym the gypsy's small tent would invite all party goers to glimpse their future.

With all this to help organize, no wonder Susie hadn't time to work up an original costume for herself. Beth apologized silently to her friend. She sighed once more in the direction of the trunk. Dick was right, she was letting it haunt her. It was probably just filled with old books and papers that would crumble when touched.

Then Elizabeth Rachel Baker, Dark-Haired Mystery Lady of Silver Maple Lane, climbed down to her room and began, rather belatedly, the Saturday ritual of room cleaning.

V

It was perfect Hallowe'en weather! Ragged pieces of cloud drifted across a moon which was obligingly full. The wind had just the right touch of chill in it as it swirled along briskly, making crisp leaves do their traditional twirling, rustling chase down the street. The bright colors of the leaves couldn't be seen at night, but their spinning and tumbling could be both seen and heard as they formed circles, scattered, and then reformed, swept along by the wind. Clouds, wind, leaves—all seemed to be hurrying to the dance and party at Shady Oaks Junior High this last Saturday in October.

Two unfamiliar figures could also be seen and heard traveling in the direction of the school. One was a clown dressed in a costume which was a combination of the harlequin trickster and the baggy-suited circus clown. The figure was basically half red and half yellow. From the neck down the right side, all was red, including a red glove and a red ballet shoe. The hat, tall and pointed, was half red and half yellow. The left side of the figure was yellow, with a yellow glove and shoe. Three large buttons, each about five inches in diameter, were sewn down the dividing line in the front. The buttons were half and half also. The difference between them was that the red half was secured on the yellow side of the costume, while the yellow showed brightly on the red. Everything was so loose and floppy that the shape of the person inside couldn't be determined. The person's hair was covered by a white cloth stretched tight and knotted under the hat, which was held on by an elastic under the chin. The harlequin touch came from the white pleated ruff around neck and wrists,

21

and from the small mask covering the top half of the face. This mask was red and yellow, in a diamond pattern.

As the figure moved quickly along, it was accompanied by another which was the exact mirror image of it! The second figure was red on the left side and yellow on the right. Gloves, shoes, ruffs, hat, and mask were identically reversed. One figure of this type alone was delightful; two were almost unbelievable. And the girls knew it. They skipped and laughed, joined hands and spun in circles with the leaves, broke apart and chased each other along. And they defied the wind to chill them, for their baggy outer costume concealed warm slacks and sweaters which could be shed when they arrived in the heated gym. They were both warm, and both disguised.

Yes, the two figures were Beth and Susie. They were in such wonderfully high spirits because they had even managed to confuse their fathers about their identities. The adults always went along with their fun, but this was the first time even they had seen the clowns together without the younger children also costumed and requiring attention. Rusty'd said aloud what everyone already knew. Even if the judges narrowed it down to Beth and Susie being the clowns, they would not easily pick which was which. He suggested that if the girls separated until after the unmasking, they might have some interesting experiences.

The girls hadn't decided yet. Enjoying each other's company and simply playing the "which is which?" game might be fun enough. But they agreed that they'd better hurry. The time spent teasing their families had already made them among the last to be traveling the streets.

As they arrived, the man who was their new principal had just begun an announcement. "At the request of Police Chief Miller, I have canceled your traditional outdoor activities. The chief feels that times have changed so much that it would be better to have you all stay on school property. Also, tonight's high wind would make a large bonfire dangerous. I know your parents and, in fact, all the people of the town, have been saving flammable rubbish for you as they do each year. Chief Miller has arranged with Mr. Lenkowski and his class in Elm Street School for a daytime clean-up on Monday.

"Of course, you're disappointed. However, your Hallowe'en Dance Committee has worked with me to give you a substitute activity which we feel can be equally enjoyable." He paused, and the bright jingling sound of a tambourine directed everyone's attention to the left side of the stage. The tambourine appeared through the curtains in a hand flashing with rings. Then a whole person burst upon them. Swirling skirts, jingling bracelets, and a half dozen golden and beaded necklaces suddenly stood next to Mr. Adams. He alone appeared unsurprised at the gypsy's rapid move from the wings to center stage.

Smiling, their principal continued, "Let me present to you an old friend of mine, Madame Clare Voyance. Madame is a true gypsy. She has consented to celebrate our holiday with us tonight. In a few minutes she and her daughter, Mademoiselle Claretta, will entertain you. Then Madame herself will spend the rest of the evening here. She will tell your fortune, if you wish. We have reserved a spot for her." He gestured toward the corner of the gym where a small, brightly colored tent had been set up. "And now..."

Again a tambourine jingled. A hand, an arm, and another entire bright, tinkling gypsy joined the first one at the footlights. The curtain parted and the two dancers began such a gay, spirited performance that everyone was immediately drawn into the party atmosphere. Some, especially the girls, considered this better than traveling up and down the dark streets dragging rubbish for a giant bonfire.

When the younger gypsy began a song about the golden earrings her lover had given her, even the boys appreciated the bittersweet tone. Her gay goodbye a while later included a wish to all of them that, "The silver coins of Good Fortune come to you." The mood was set for an evening of vagabond fun.

Beth and Susie decided to stay together. They were heading for the punch bowl when they were met by a pirate and a tramp who suggested that the punch would taste much better after a dance or two.

It was a half hour later when they finally did get a drink and an orange cupcake. They stood side by side talking about the costumed figures dancing by. "It looks like Eva will get the prize for prettiest again this year," said Beth. "She always is some sort of fairy princess. That long blonde hair of hers is a lovely asset. Her costume is more or less the same each year, just a different color. Pastel green, pale blue, soft peach. That filmy lavender tonight looks like pieces of clouds. If only she were as sweet as she looks."

"I think Jessy has a lot to do with how Eva acts. Eva is sort of shy. She lives near Jessy and they walk to school together. Jessy wants to be popular like her cousin Marilyn. She isn't pretty, but she has snap and style. She needs a friend and Eva needs confidence. They support each other," observed Susie.

"They deserve each other, too," said Beth, more unkindly than she usually spoke. "I just don't like those two. They make me feel as if something unpleasant will happen if I associate with them."

"I don't feel especially warm toward them either, Beth. But we don't have to be concerned. We have our own crowd. Say, let's take advantage of the chance to have our fortunes told. The crowd around Madame's tent has thinned quite a bit. We shouldn't have to wait too long for a turn. What do you say?"

"Good idea," answered Beth.

The clowns made their way to the corner of the gym and joined a cowboy, a witch, and a ghost waiting outside the small tent. The witch, it appeared, had already been in and was telling the others about her experience.

"I thought she'd just read my palm. From out here it looks as if there is only room for two chairs inside. But she's really serious. There's a small round table with a black cloth on it, and she has a deck of about eighty cards. They all have pictures on them, and fancy symbols. Swords, five pointed stars, things like that. The pictures of people aren't just kings and queens, there are ordinary people, and magicians, and soldiers, and priests...."

Just then a colonial lady came out of the tent and the ghost went in.

"Golly!" exclaimed the cowboy. "What was it like in there, Alice?"

"Very interesting," answered the colonial lady. She took up the story where the witch had been interrupted. "She has a lot of fancy cards and she asks the real color of your hair and eyes. Then she chooses a card to represent you and has you shuffle the deck. She turns cards over one by one and puts them over and around your card in a special pattern. She's very serious, but not at all scary. She told me I could be good at music, but I must practice long and hard. I've been told that lots of times before, guess we all have. Being told by a real gypsy on Hallowe'en is fun, though. I enjoyed it."

24

As the ghost came out, the cowboy said, "Somebody else go next. I don't think I'll bother." He walked away with Alice.

Susie was closest to the entrance, so she slipped in. Beth was left with the witch and ghost. When a tramp and a pirate came along, witch and ghost drifted away. Beth began telling the new arrivals what she'd heard from those who had been into the tent already. She was interrupted by Bill, the pirate. He exclaimed, "Why, those are Tarot cards! This should be interesting!"

"What do you know about Tarot cards?" asked Beth.

"I'm far from an authority, but I was looking up something about cards in the encyclopedia last week and came across the entry about Tarot. I was curious, so I read it through. It said nobody knows for sure where they came from. Some say Egypt because the symbols are a lot like hieroglyphics. Others say the Chinese invented them. The Chinese invented just about everything, if you believe some stories. Others say the gypsies brought them from India, and still others count the Hebrews in. Some of the letters are like the Hebrew alphabet. It all adds up to interesting, though, doesn't it?"

Beth was delighted. "It sure does! I can hardly wait."

"Well, you'll have to wait 'til Beth comes out, that's for sure," said Bill.

"Hey, you mean until Susie comes out. That's Beth we're talking to," declared Bob. The tramp turned toward her. "Right?" he asked.

But Beth just giggled. This was absolutely the best Hallowe'en she'd ever had!

Just then the tent flap opened, Susie stepped out and Beth slipped past her, leaving her friend to cope with the puzzled boys.

VI

There really was very little room inside the tent. Beth's tall pointed hat brushed the canvas and she sat down quickly on the empty stool opposite the gypsy. The round table between them was less than two feet in diameter. It was covered with a black cloth which hung in folds to within six inches of the floor. The space inside the tent was lit from beneath the table. She learned later from Susie that a flashlight was suspended beneath the table to shine downwards, and the light reflected from the waxed gym floor. It made a dim but pleasant glow.

"Ah, what a clever costume. You and your friend must surely win a prize tonight." Madame Clare smiled at Beth. "But you are a very different person from her. The vibrations are not at all alike," Madame continued. "She is alive and active; you are quiet and dreaming."

"Wow!" exclaimed Beth. "I walk in and nearly knock off my hat and you can tell all that!"

"I can tell many things. But you must tell me your complexion before I select the correct querent card for you. All you young people are pages. There are four different ones, though. Which one represents you depends on several different things," explained Madame.

The gypsy continued, "Since tonight is for enjoyment more than for serious problems, I will just tell you a few things. You are dark? The stars, then. Pentangles. Shuffle the cards, dear. Now cut them and make three piles." Madame had chosen a card picturing a young person holding and studying a ball with a five pointed star on it. She placed cards in a pattern around it. Then she began.

"You have many stars and cups. The stars are diamonds for wealth. The cups are hearts for love and friendship. This ten shows a happy family. And here is a five—a good friend. Ah ha, a treasure in your house, high up! But you have not good health, for your major star is upside down. And you can be stubborn...not entirely bad, to be stubborn. One must be determined and somewhat stubborn to win a treasure and keep a friend. You have a good future, little one. Go now and be happy with your family and friends."

Madame smiled at her and began gathering the cards. Beth realized she was being dismissed. She muttered her thanks, stood up and then immediately stooped. Her hat had hit the tent again. As she ducked out, the brightness of the gym blinded her for a moment. Then she saw Susie waiting and they walked away together.

After hearing Beth's fortune, Susie declared, "If there is anything to this at all, I'd be surprised. She said I had a good friend, too. And she'd have to be heavy on family because we kids aren't old enough to be on our own. Of course, it's just meant to be a fun evening, but with the two of us dressed alike, she'd be sure we were friends."

"Madame didn't know there were two of us dressed alike until she saw me, though," Beth pointed out. "Whatever she said to you about a friend wasn't because of our great costuming. She told me there was a treasure in my house, high up. I'll bet it's that trunk! She also said I had to be determined and stubborn. Susie, my good friend, won't you be stubborn and determined with me and help me find the treasure in the trunk?"

Susie laughed. "Well, OK. But really because of the adventurous spirit Madame said I had. I'll talk up a Grand Trunk Opening with you. But remember, words of prophecy can be interpreted many ways. A treasure up high could be an emerald ring in a trunk in an attic or it could be pie in the sky!"

Alice and Cowboy Joe hurried up to them just then. "C'mon, you two. They've called for the contestants in the costume parade. We're anxious to see if anyone can tell which of you is which. Everyone knows you're Susie and Beth, of course. And you are both great. Now it's time for the whole truth!"

The girls were glad to have Alice in their crowd. She seldom competed in anything, but she always enjoyed the school activities. She made posters and sold tickets and came out and cheered every event. She'd probably get a prize when she graduated, in spite of herself. The one for school spirit.

The clowns joined the large circle of costumed students in the center of the gym. Mr. Adams and several parents were judges. Madame Clare had been invited to be a judge. While she couldn't help identify, she certainly could vote as an authority on costume quality. And she'd be impartial, too.

Each participant could compete in only one group. The girls had chosen best disguise rather than original or funny.

The contestants circled the gym so everyone could see and enjoy them. That way the judges got a good look at them, too. The witch was chosen scariest. When unmasked she proved to be one of the new students from Ashwood. The girls didn't know her well. Eva did indeed win for prettiest, and Bob's tramp outfit was declared most authentic. After several others had won and unmasked, those who hadn't won in their particular group dropped out.

Finally there were only the clowns and a ghost left to be identified. Since only prize winners were unmasked, the ghost still had a chance. The girls put the ghost between them, and all three stood before the judges. There was a general buzzing as the crowd in the gym shared their unofficial decisions with each other.

Suddenly Jessy, from the sidelines, took off her mask and ran over to Susie. "C'mon, Susie Benson, I know it's you! I've listened to your voice every chance I got tonight."

Everyone looked at Mr. Adams. He conferred with his judges a moment and then said, "We still aren't sure. It's just a guess, but we'll go with Jessy. The clown she calls Susie, please take off your mask."

Susie and Beth both managed smiles as they removed masks, hats, and hair coverings. The applause was for them as much as for the ghost who had won. The winner revealed himself to be a timid fellow with thick glasses. His face was familiar to everyone, but few knew that his name was Alfred. It didn't matter much, however, for from then on he was Casper.

All masks were then removed and the party continued for a while. Each winner was surrounded by a group of friends congratulating him and admiring his prize. Anyone who cared to notice would have seen that Eva did not pay much attention to Jessy. In fact, Jessy was quite alone until Casper asked her to dance. Until an hour ago, he would not have dared to approach her. And, until an hour ago, Jessy would not have accepted.

On the way home, Beth kicked at the fallen leaves and grumbled, "I know the prize isn't all that important, but Jessy really is bad news. Will you admit that much, Susie?"

"Bad news for us, yes. I think Casper sees her in another light, though. Besides, we had fun fooling people. Maybe your prize will be that pie in the sky I promised to help you find."

Beth brightened, "Right. That could be even better. I hope it will be cocoanut custard, that's my favorite!"

Susie laughed, "And I'll share gladly. Both the search and the pie. Seriously, see you tomorrow for some plotting and planning?"

"OK. Call me."

The girls parted and disappeared into their own homes, and the crisp autumn leaves chased each other down the street undisturbed.

VII

It was early afternoon of the second Sunday in November and Beth and Susie were sitting on Beth's bed trying to wait calmly for one more hour. This was the day of the Grand Trunk Opening.

"Funny, isn't it, that it was Joey, finally, who helped us," said Beth for the hundredth time.

Susie agreed, for the hundredth time, and then added, "She really is growing up, I guess. Also, her teacher is new here this year, and she seems to be making American History very interesting for Joey."

"How's that?"

"Well, they do projects like making things the colonists could have used. They pretend they are living the events they study, then make up letters and diaries giving first person accounts. They draw maps and put the early names of places on. Camden was once Cooper's Ferry, Joey told us," explained Susie.

"So that's the answer," said Beth. "I was in the kitchen one afternoon when Joey came over to read Mom something she'd written. When she heard about the trunk, she spent the rest of the afternoon coaxing Mom to open it."

"She's now convinced the folks to have a sort of family affair like the one she was too young to really enjoy five years ago. Remember, when all that work was done to your second floor?" continued Susie.

Beth smiled, "We did have a good time that winter, didn't we?" Then she sobered a bit. "It almost seems as if this is Joey's day instead of mine. Then again, that's not a bad idea. If there is no valuable treasure in the trunk, we will have had a good time today, anyhow."

"Why, Beth," Susie sounded surprised, "that's the first time I've ever heard you even hint that the trunk might not hold something special!"

"Well, we'll know soon," replied Beth, brightening as she heard the voices of the Bensons in the kitchen. There followed almost immediately the sound of footsteps.

The two girls got into the hall just in time to meet Joey running up the last few steps, calling the obvious, "We're here!" The boys came next, each carrying some part of the equipment Bud had brought. Dick had the tool box, while Rusty and Tom had cans of oil, rust remover, and rags.

Dick glanced at his father for a nod before pulling down the stairs. He held them steady while the girls and his brothers climbed, then followed quickly.

As soon as the six pairs of jeans and sneakers had disappeared, Bud went up to supervise. He had promised the girls he'd make sure the Feline Defenders of the Future did as little damage as possible to the remnants of the past.

Pops, in old pants and sweatshirt that had paint smears from every room in both houses, was patiently waiting while his wife got a scarf for Joy Benson's hair. He would stay down until both moms had climbed safely.

Beth enjoyed and appreciated the fact that her mother had entered into the spirit of the day by tying a bandana around her head, knotting it in front. This made her look like the figure on the tee shirt they'd given her. This pictured a smiling woman waving a broom and dust cloth and was labeled WORLD'S CLEANEST MOM. However, Beth now squirmed with impatience at the delay caused by Mom's trying to keep Joy clean, too.

At last they were all up. The attic ran the whole length of the house, so that although the roof slanted, there was plenty of room for all ten to stand straight.

They were all surprisingly silent. The females were just standing around. Dick and Tom rubbed at the lock, Rusty oiled the hinges. Bud examined the leather handles. Pops was watching and thinking; he seemed to be trying to remember something.

"One of these handles is broken," Bud noted. "The edges at the break are still sharp, so it's most likely been done recently."

Tom explained, "Well, when we found this trunk about six weeks ago, I tried pulling it by the handle. It moved about two feet, and then the leather tore. It was under the eaves by the chimney there," he pointed, then continued. "It was too dark to see well, plus there wasn't room to open it over there. So we moved it."

"Yeah," continued Dick, "it was pretty hard work, too. Took all three of us, pushing and shoving. Sorry we scraped the floor, Mom," he added, glancing at Bess.

"That's it!" exclaimed Pops suddenly. "That's Belle's trunk!"

"Belle's trunk? Who's Belle?" Beth asked excitedly. Her hopes soared.

Pops thought aloud, "Belle... Belle... Isabelle? Anabelle? Your great grandmother, Belle Jefferson...."

"Jefferson. Jefferson! Did she have red hair?" Joey mirrored Beth's excitement. "Maybe there's a picture of her inside. Remember the albums we found in Granny's trunk, Susie? Those funny 1920 bathing suits at Atlantic City. There was enough material in one to make a dozen bikinis!"

Everyone laughed at the thought.

"This trunk is much older than Granny Benson's, dear," her mother explained. "How old would it be, Pops?" she turned to her neighbor.

"Could be close to a hundred years. I don't remember Belle very well. She was nearly seventy when I was born. Died when I was only five or six. My sister Ann was closer to her. Ann was about Beth's age when Belle died. The thing I remember most about her death was how Ann cried. You know how it is, most of what you think you remember from when you're young is really family history that's been repeated so often you think you remember being there.

"I know she was born in Virginia. Came to live with us in Egg Harbor when Grandfather Baker died. She was a grandmother, but everyone called her Belle."

Bess Baker laughed, "That's a story your mother was fond of telling, Tom. She was looking forward to welcoming a sweet, white-haired mother-in-law who would sit in her own mother's rocker in the bay window and tell the children stories of the Old South."

All work on the trunk had stopped, as the children in the Bakers' attic, and Bud and Joy as well, turned to listen.

"Mary Baker had met Will's mother at the wedding, but since then had been so busy having children and taking care of her own sick parents, that aside from Christmas cards and birth announcements, there had been very little communication between them.

"So, when this lively lady appeared, walking up the front steps, and Mary greeted her as Mother Baker, they were all told quite gaily, 'Belle, please, dear. Call me Belle. Mother Baker sounds so domestic! Everyone, call me Belle.'"

Beth was delighted, "What else, Mom? Can you remember anything else about her?"

"Actually, anything I'd remember would be hearsay. Belle's been dead more than thirty years. Your Aunt Ann was the one closest to her. Belle must have been a very dynamic person, though. I'm calling her Belle, now, myself!"

Susie asked, "How did her trunk get into your attic, though, Aunt Bess? If she lived in Virginia and died in Egg Harbor?"

"I've been trying to figure that one out myself," said Pops.

Rusty, who had been rubbing the metal parts of the trunk with oil, suggested quietly, "There may be some sort of clue here. This looks like a name plate."

"We didn't bring polish, but maybe you can get a rubbing with this piece of wrapping paper and a pencil, Rusty," said Bud.

"Oh, boy! Like from tombstones," Joey cried.

"Dear child!" exclaimed Joy.

Rusty worked quickly, and soon handed a paper to Pops. "Thomas Baker—1882" Pops read the name and date aloud. "Well, let's see now..."

Bud interrupted, "May I suggest that we keep at the lock? This conversation is most interesting, but we can surely listen and work at the same time."

"A worthy recommendation," agreed Pops. "Time is moving along."

The boys stepped away and let Bud at the lock—which, they knew, was what he'd meant.

Pops continued thinking aloud. "My grandfather, I've been told, was eight or ten years older than Belle. This could have been his trunk. If so, she brought it from Virginia for sentimental reasons. When she died, Frank and I were moved into her rooms. When Frank married and built his own house, I had the place to myself until you and I were married, Bess."

"We were only there a few months," Bess reminded him.

"Right. And when we moved here, we had a dozen or so relatives and friends helping us. Someone must have managed to read the name on the trunk and load it onto Frank's truck."

"And when we got here?" asked Bess.

"A couple of your cousins wrestled it up to the attic and stowed it under the eaves," finished Dick.

"They must have been first cousins to Hercules!" remarked Tom, still conscious of the broken leather handle.

Bud laughed, "They were probably just good, strong South Jersey farmers." Then he added, "There's no saving this lock, though, my friends. It's too old and rusted. What I suggest is to try to unscrew the whole thing from the trunk."

"Whatever you think, Bud."

32

"Pops, why did you get Belle's rooms instead of Aunt Ann? I'd have thought that if she loved Belle so, Aunt Ann would have liked them," Beth asked.

"Well, again, I was so young at the time.... But I think it was the suddenness of her death and the shock to Ann. If Belle had been sick in bed for a time and Ann had spent hours at her side, the room would have held gentler memories. I believe our parents knew Frank and I would soon change the whole tone of the place."

"How did she die?" asked Rusty.

"Belle was a wonderfully healthy person, and it was a great shock to everyone when, in 1942, she slipped on a small rug and struck her head on the corner of the bed. We all heard her fall, but she was dead when Dad got to her."

The simplicity of Pops' account and the brevity of the statement sent a new shock through the group in the attic.

"You know," mused Joey, "I was about to say, 'Poor Belle.' But she didn't suffer long in dying, and she's not been forgotten, because here we all are talking about her...."

"And smiling," added Susie.

"How about, 'Poor Aunt Ann?'" asked Beth.

Bess Baker considered that one. "I'd say not that either. Anytime I've heard Ann mention Belle it has been with pleasure. And with a smile. Ann outgrew her tragic teens, as most of us do. She has a home and family of her own now."

"And we have a ninety-five-year-old trunk..." Bud stood dramatically. "Unlocked!"

VIII

A glad shout, accompanied by applause and a whistle or two, burst from the group. Those who had been lounging on the boxes and furniture in the attic stood up, and there was a general surge of movement toward the trunk.

Bud, who was not what people would call a tall man, had a manner of authority about him. He knew himself and he knew his work. He was secure in the fact that he was a fine craftsman. His family and friends loved and respected him. His gesture of standing and holding up the lock, for example, was a natural one. It had the dramatic effect he had tried for, and everyone responded to it. Their attention was again focused on the trunk, rather than on the events in the Baker family history.

With all now on their feet, Bud brought his arm down in a sweeping gesture. He indicated the trunk, turned toward his neighbor, and while bowing from the waist, proclaimed, "Your property, Mr. Baker...."

There was for Beth another delay while Pops returned Bud's bow. "I thank you, my friend. My wife thanks you. My daughter thanks you. My three sons thank you..."

"Oh, please!" Beth simply couldn't keep still another minute. "Please, Pops, open it!"

Pops turned toward her. "How about helping me, Princess?" he invited. "Here we go."

Beth eagerly stepped up, and the two lifted the lid to disclose a broad brimmed lady's hat, which was decorated by an ostrich feather. The lifting of the lid stirred the feather, and it waved gently. Pops reached in, took the hat, and placed it on Beth's dark curls.

Her mother clasped both hands over her heart in mock admiration, as she declared, "Why, my dear, that's just the thing to wear to the wedding. Those Yankees will know their little Mary Adams is getting a fine Virginia gentleman when his mama arrives in this!" Then she reached out to tilt the hat over Beth's right eye.

Joy gathered up the feather boa which had been lying under the hat. "This is an absolute must," she said, as she draped it around the young girl's shoulders.

"As is your purse, madame," added Bud, playing along. He handed Beth a small purse, beautifully decorated. Tiny beads had been sewn in a flower pattern over the whole surface. There was a beaded fringe on the bottom and a gold chain attached to the sides of the frame, which curved to form a clasp closing.

Beth put one hand on her hip, and with the beaded purse dangling from the fingers of her other hand, struck a pose.

"Oh," squirmed Joey in delight, "do you think Belle really wore those?"

Dick laughed, "It's for sure Tom didn't!"

"Oh, you!" Joey tossed her head, then pulled from the trunk a straw hat with a faded ribbon around the crown. "I'll bet he wore this, though," she said, handing it to the nearest boy. That was Rusty, who obligingly put on the hat and posed next to his sister.

"This cane surely goes with it," Susie joined the game now, picking up a bamboo colored stick with a hook like a candy cane.

"Can you picture us as the parents of the groom?" asked Beth.

Pops looked at the two children. Rusty had one arm around his sister's waist. His other hand held the cane out at an angle, the bottom resting on the floor next to his foot. He bent his knee and cocked his head as if flirting with the feathered lady and her beaded purse. "Well," Pops considered, "more along the lines of a Norman Rockwell print, I'd say."

"A striped blazer would put them on the boardwalk in Atlantic City," volunteered Joy.

"Or they could be a song and dance team from an old vaudeville show," suggested Bess. "Remember the 'Strolling through the Park' routines?"

Meanwhile the other children were taking items of clothing from the trunk and trying them on. Soon the adults joined in. They admired each other, exchanged clothes, and admired again.

Susie laughed. "This looks like Hallowe'en all over again. Don't you wish we'd found these in time?"

"No, indeed! I wouldn't have missed our twin clowns for anything," declared Bud. "Wish I could've made it to the party and seen you in action!"

"We can probably use some of these for next year, though," Pops remarked. "Notice they're very well preserved? They're different ages, too. The various styles span thirty or forty years."

"Any idea why?" Joy asked.

Bess thought aloud, "Maybe Great Grandfather Baker was concerned about his appearance. We know he was a lawyer, and a prosperous one. If he knew the importance of looking well and could afford it, he'd have his clothes custom made. So, they'd go out of style before they wore out. He just didn't throw them away."

"I've been hoping for Belle's wedding dress to turn up," Beth confessed.

Her brother Tom reminded her, "This was really Tom's trunk, wasn't it?"

"Yes," agreed Beth, "but there's other things of Belle's here."

"Well then," continued Tom, "did she have daughters? They may have worn it for their weddings. Do girls do such things, or do they want their own 'specially made gowns?"

"Belle did have daughters. Twins. I never met my aunts, though," his father answered.

Joey spoke up, "I've heard of the bride wearing her mother's veil, but not her gown. Maybe they're not the same size, so the gown wouldn't fit."

"Ah ha!" cried Dick, who had been silent until now. "I figured there must be more than old clothes in this trunk to make it so heavy."

"The eternal scientist," remarked Susie, in a voice which was a cross between friendly and proud.

Tom asked his brother, "Whadda ya have, pal?"

"The bottom half of this seems to be full of books. Looks like a whole law library!"

Just at that moment Rusty turned to Pops. "I seem to have found something in the inside pocket here." He had on what looked like the oldest vest and coat of all. It hung somewhat loosely on him, and the material was not as expensive as other suits in the trunk. In fact, it looked to be homespun. "Some kind of notebook, seems like," Rusty added as he handed over his find.

As it exchanged hands, something fell out of the covers. Beth stooped to pick it up, but gave her attention to Pops and what Rusty had found in the vest pocket of the old suit.

"This seems to be a daily account book. Odds and ends of notes and numbers. Much is faded and blurred. What did you pick up, Beth?"

"This is an envelope, I can feel papers inside. There's writing on the outside, too," Beth answered, as she passed the envelope to her father.

Pops read, "'Thomas Francis Baker' is the name here. There's a date. Let's see." He tilted the envelope to get a better light on it. "'September 8, 1882.'"

"Look, friends," Bess Baker interrupted, "we've been here a couple of hours now. How about taking this envelope and the notebook downstairs? We can continue our historical research over snacks in the comfort of the kitchen."

Four voices crying, "Oh, Mah-ahm!" spoke aloud the message in the pleading looks from the other children. Then all six turned to Pops.

"Most of us really are curious to get to the bottom of the

trunk, Bess," he said. With a glance at the others, he bargained, "If we empty the trunk and don't stop to read or inspect, we can satisfy our curiosity. We'll bring down anything else that looks interesting, alright?"

Bess answered, "Well, alright." Then she added, "We don't have to stop at all. I'm enjoying this, too, but it's getting late, and a bit chilly up here. I just thought you'd all like a break. There aren't many things that can take the children's minds off food for so long a time!"

Everyone laughed. Joy glanced at her watch and then at the window, which showed the November afternoon giving way to a windy evening. "Suppose we do start to stop? Bess and I could go down and set up in the kitchen. The rest of you could check out whatever is still in the trunk. And, please, do bring down any other interesting things."

As both mothers left, the children went back to the trunk and began emptying it. The boys handed out books, and the girls stacked them on the floor. These youngsters had so often worked and played together that they anticipated each others' moves. Today, however, in an unconscious acceptance of Joey's growing up, they paired off.

Rusty worked with Beth. They both were interested in reading titles and leafing through the books, so they were the slowest.

Dick and Susie seemed more concerned with producing an empty trunk than in checking things removed.

Tom and Joey worked steadily, but Joey tried to sort the books into sizes as she went along. Tom humored her by handing her one at a time. He admitted to himself, though, that this gave him time to see if a diary or journal was among them.

It also gave him time to remark, "I've been thinking, Belle didn't want to be Mother Baker, but our mom sure fits the title."

"You're right, son," agreed Pops. "That's one of the special things about her. She makes sure that everyone around her is as comfortable as possible."

"Double right," interrupted Dick, standing abruptly. "And now that we see there's nothing more here, let's head for the kitchen and all that great comfort."

"And leave the attic like this!" cried Beth. "All the clothes around, and the books on the floor...."

Dick turned on his sister, "I don't believe you care anything about neatness! You're still dumb enough to insist there's a great

37

treasure here. A pearl necklace? Spanish doubloons? Maybe the emerald tiara Queen Isabella gave to Pocahontas?"

Beth shouted back, "How would you know what's here? You've been shoveling stuff out so fast."

Tom tried to distract them, "Hey, Isabella lived a century before Pocahontas, didn't she?"

"And Raleigh took his Indian princess to England, not Spain," Joey butted in with her new knowledge.

Dick was still annoyed, "Who cares? They're all dead now!"

"OK. That's it." Pops took over. "Rusty, you help the girls bring over the empty cartons we use for winter clothes. They can put the suits and dresses in them. Tom and Dick, gather up Bud's tools and take them downstairs. I'll explain to Bess about the books on the floor. All of you have my permission to come up whenever you have a chance and go through them carefully. Put each book in the trunk after you've finished with it. If you find anything you want to read, you can bring it down. Let's go."

Tom and Dick easily packed up and went with Bud to put his equipment in his garage workshop. The girls and Rusty soon had the clothes safely in the cartons, and climbed downstairs. Pops gave the attic a final quick check before following the others.

Within a short time all ten were seated in "Mother Baker's" warm kitchen, chatting about the unexpected costume party they'd enjoyed in the attic.

Beth wisely kept silent. Her strong feelings about the trunk and its treasure seemed to disturb her parents more and more. Thinking back, she realized that the arguments she'd had with Dick were all centered around her interest in the trunk, too. Still, she wasn't convinced they'd found everything of value that was there.

IX

To everyone's surprise, it was Bess Baker who asked to have the envelope opened. They had finished eating and had cleared the table, but were all feeling there was, somehow, more to come.

Bess sat down with a sigh, saying, "Thank goodness and you, Pops, for modern kitchen equipment. The dishes are being washed and fresh coffee is being made. I can relax with everyone

38

else while you read whatever is in Beth's envelope."

Without further delay, Pops carefully unfolded the sheets of paper. In spite of his caution, one split across the crease. "This is very fragile. The writing is clear enough. Lots of flourishes. If it proves worth keeping, maybe we can slip it in one of those plastic folders you children use for term papers." He then spread the sheets flat on the table, adjusted his glasses, and began:

Dear Tom,

You have always known that your mother died when you were a baby. Although you never asked, you must have wondered about her and about your father. Because you are such a loving and thoughtful person, you may have felt that asking about them would make us think you didn't love us. Whatever the reason, I'm going to make their story my gift to you.

Bob and Thomas made the trunk, and Mr. Steward engraved the name plate. The girls sewed a good suit for you. You will get them all before you read this, so I'm not giving away any of the surprises they have planned for your birthday and farewell party tonight. This letter and the package I'll hand you tomorrow. You can read on the train.

February 24, 1862 was a clear, cold day. The war was less than a year old, and here in the hills we weren't much worried about it. So, when we heard the knock on the door just before supper, Thomas opened it right away.

I remember as if it were yesterday. There stood the prettiest girl I'd ever seen! Even cold and lost looking, blue eyed Ann with her long dark curls was lovely.

She was Thomas's cousin from New Jersey, and after we got her warm and fed, she told us what the war had done to her life. It was a sad story, but I've always been glad about it. It brought you both into our lives and gave us each other to love.

Ann told us that she and a young man named Frank Baker had grown up together in Egg Harbor. Everyone there knew that some day they'd marry. Frank cared a great deal about Abe Lincoln and the Union. Even though he was only eighteen when the shooting started, he felt he just must go and fight. But he also cared a great deal for Ann. She was even younger than Frank, but she knew her mind, too. She wanted Frank.

Both families disapproved, but in early December, they got married. Ann was an only child, as was Frank. However, when she prepared to share Frank's home just down the street at...

Pops interrupted himself, "That's the torn part. I can't make out the address and the next line." Then he continued:

...father shouted that if she left then she'd never be allowed back.

Frank planned to enlist after the holidays, and Ann had a hard time convincing him not to go right then and leave her with her own family until after the war.

Frank's parents were not unkind to her. However, when news of his death came in early February, they were so grief stricken themselves, they made no attempt to comfort Ann.

That first night she didn't tell us the details of her journey to us in West Virginia. She just said she knew Tom and Edna McCloskey would help her. Later we never bothered to ask.

She was here nearly a month before she realized you were coming. By then spring rains and thaw, war time travel dangers, and the uncertainty of her reception in New Jersey all worked against her leaving. Mainly, we'd all grown so happy together none of us seriously considered parting.

I'm spending so many words on our love for her and for you because I want you to know, and carry through your life, the knowledge that you have a caring family.

You were born on September 8, 1862. Ann was delighted! She had been pretty as a cold, hungry traveler in the winter. She was radiant as a new mother. She named you Thomas Francis. My Thomas had given you a home; her Frank had given you life.

She tried then to contact your grandparents to tell them of your birth. When she got no answer, she chose to blame war conditions.

Thomas and I made another attempt to contact them when Ann died of a fever a week before your second birthday. To tell the truth, I'm glad we failed. I don't know how I'd have given you up. It's hard even now, Tom, to see you go. But I tell myself a chance to train with a successful lawyer in Richmond is not to be lost.

One more thing, Ann trusted me with a package. A small velvet box wrapped in oilskin. She said Frank gave it to her as a wedding present. It had gone to the first born Baker in every generation for a hundred years. She didn't say what it was, though. I'm giving it to you as you leave. May it be of help to you, dear boy. You seem so young. Remember you always have a home here.

Go with my blessing, and have a long, prosperous life.

Lovingly,
Edna

Susie was the first to speak. "That's a really beautiful letter. It's like the Christmas shows on TV. I wish Edna were an ancestor of mine."

"Where exactly did you find this?" asked Bud, of no one in particular.

Rusty answered, "It was in an inside pocket of the jacket I had on. That and a notebook. I didn't feel anything else in any pocket, though. I didn't try the pants on, but when we were putting the clothes in cartons later, I checked the whole suit especially."

"I'm sure there's nothing left in the trunk," Dick volunteered. "I admit I was hurrying, but I really made sure the trunk was completely empty."

Tom spoke up, too. "Yes, we three are thorough workers. I vouch for the emptiness, too."

"Well, Pops, you said we could look through the books again. May we also go through the carton and the pockets of the clothes?" Beth asked.

"You lookin' for an oilskin packet in a book?" shot Dick. "Maybe he had to sell it to get his practice started."

Beth managed not to comment, but looked to her parents for the permission she'd requested. They were speculating about the packet.

"Maybe he gave it to Belle and it's been passed to one of their children," suggested Joy.

"The oldest child would be my father," said Pops. "His oldest is my brother Bill. Bill never married."

"No!" cried Beth spontaneously. "I'm sure it's in our attic."

41

"Please, Beth," her mother frowned. "You worry me. You may indeed search some more, but not tonight. All you children have school tomorrow."

"And I have a letter to write," declared Joey.

Susie turned a shocked face to her sister, "You're not going to use the people we've talked about here in one of your class reports!"

'Course not. Besides, we're only up to the War of 1812. I want to tell Dan. Let's both write, Susie. You tell about Ann and Edna, because you liked them so much. I'll write about Belle. I'll bet she did have red hair."

So, soon Joey and Susie were bundled warmly for the short trip across the yard. The adults prepared to take their coffee into the living room and relax on the easy chairs around the coffee table there. The Baker children headed upstairs.

For an instant Joey's bright face reappeared around the front door, as she proclaimed, "Thanks, everybody! The whole day was just super!"

X

Beth gazed out the classroom window. It was after lunch on the last Tuesday in November, and Thanksgiving holidays began at noon tomorrow. It had just begun to snow.

"Beth?" The tone of Mrs. Gardiner's voice calling her name seemed to imply that the teacher, too, had holiday thoughts.

Searching her memory swiftly for the question, Beth's mind suddenly clicked with an added thought. "Why...West Virginia!" she answered.

"Why not?" quipped Mike Helme, class clown.

Mrs. Gardiner joined in the laughter. "Alright, class. Take a minute or two to look at the snow. But then we'll really have to continue the lesson. This is the last time we'll meet before next Monday, and we'll be glad to have completed this unit. We can start a new one with the new week."

By the time school was dismissed, the big, spectacular flakes that had distracted their favorite teacher's class had changed to smaller, steadily falling ones that seemed to mean business. Beth and Susie were walking home.

The first snow of the year was always exciting, but Beth seemed to be especially delighted. She ran and kicked, scooped up handfuls and threw them in the air, then jumped aside so she wouldn't be showered with it. "You're all wound up, Beth. What makes you act so silly?" asked her friend.

"I feel silly, oh, so silly," sang Beth, as she continued her spiraling down the street. Then she stopped, caught her breath, and laughingly counted on her fingers, "Bunches of things. First, I have a chance to be out in the beautiful snow. Second, our holidays begin tomorrow. Also, I got an idea in history that will be fun to check out. AND, we'll have a great holiday, being all together, because Dan's coming home.... When's he due, Susie?"

"Not until tomorrow, actually," Susie answered. "His last class is today, but he's staying to finish a paper for one of his courses. That way he won't have it on his mind during the visit, and he'll still have all day to fly home."

"Dan's really terrific, if I do say so," declared Beth.

Susie laughed, "You're allowed to say so. Everyone does."

"I noticed. Sometimes I think he's almost too good to be true. Uncle Bud is so proud of him, and Aunt Joy seems to have a special understanding where he's concerned. You and Joey don't argue with him the way I do with Dick, either. He has lots of friends in town, too."

"Well, to begin with, Dan's a lot older than Joey and me. Dick's your kid brother. I've noticed you don't argue with Tom or Rusty the way you do with Dick. Especially lately," Susie pointed out. "Any clue why?"

"No, except most of our trouble seems to be over my insisting there's a treasure in our attic."

"Has anyone been up to look through the books and other clothes yet?" asked Susie.

"I haven't heard anyone say. I got halfway up the steps once, but Mom called to ask me to go supermarket shopping with her. She had an extra long list and would need two carts. Stuff for the Thanksgiving dinner. I'm glad you're all coming over, instead of us going to relatives, or something," Beth declared.

Susie agreed.

They had reached their own homes by now, so separated until their walk to school in the morning.

No one, not even Jack Pierce, the Precision Predictor on TV, expected so much snow on Tuesday night. It wasn't a howling storm, to attract attention to itself, just a steadily falling snow that came and came all night long. "Like Asian hordes overrunning Europe," suggested Rusty.

On Wednesday morning the radio and TV were broadcasting school closings. Beth was tempted just to turn over and go back to sleep, when the phone rang. It was Susie. She said Bud was taking all the children on the block to the rink to ice skate at about ten o'clock. The parents liked the idea because it kept everyone together and indoors. It sounded good to Beth, too.

However, when the time came she'd changed her mind. This would be an ideal chance to go to the attic. No boys to disturb her. Pops at work. Mom busy in the kitchen. As soon as Bud's van was out of sight, Beth went down to tell her mother where she'd be.

"Alright, but put on a sweater," said Mom. "If you must go," she added, over her shoulder.

Beth turned to leave, but stopped when she heard the clatter of falling pans, followed by her mother's almost tearful, "Oh, dear...."

"Mom! What is it?... Are you alright?" Beth hurried back.

"Oh, I suppose so," Bess answered. "There's just so much to do, and I thought for a minute you were coming to help. Then, instead, I see all you think of is gypsies and treasures." She was stooping to gather up the pans, so Beth couldn't see her face, but the tone of her mother's voice carried a worried sadness that was unfamiliar.

Beth bent to help. "I'm sorry, Mom. I am being selfish. Come to think of it, having the five Bensons over pretty much doubles the load. This isn't the same as the snacks we often have together. Even then, Aunt Joy helps. What can I do? Polish some silver or give you a hand with the baking?"

"Well, yes," Mom's smile was beautiful. "Baking is what needs doing most. I'm planning for two cakes and several dozen cookies, if possible."

Beth moved to gather the bowls and ingredients she'd need. "I enjoy baking. Maybe our name came from some ancestor who was a master baker in a medieval town, and every generation or so the urge pops up."

"You are quite interested in family background, aren't you? I never noticed it much until you became obsessed with that old trunk," remarked Bess, who was now bent over the sink.

44

"Guess it does seem an obsession," admitted the young girl. "Let me try to explain, though. OK?" She looked up to catch her mother's nod, then continued.

"Well, I'm finding out that I've done more reading than many of the other kids in my class, even Susie. Lots of things our teachers tell us I already have heard about, but it's big news to the others.

"So, when people told me I was making up a good bit of my ideas about the trunk, that it was wishful thinking combined with romantic novels, I almost wanted to believe them. Yet, from the very first day I saw it, I've had a special feeling about that trunk. Almost as if it had a magnet inside, attracting me. I guess I did pester everybody.

"But then, when Pops read the letter about the oilskin packet, I felt there wasn't a terribly great hurry anymore. Whatever is in the packet, it's not going away. We mustn't give up the idea of finding it, though. Dick seems to want to do that...."

Bess Baker looked up then. "Yes, he worries me, too. I'd say he was afraid, but that's not it."

"I've no idea what Dick's problem is, but I'm glad you mentioned it," continued Beth, as she cracked eggs and beat them in a small separate bowl. "We either argue or don't talk to each other at all anymore.

"But that's about it, Mom. Sometime we've got to go searching for the packet. I'd thought today was a good time, as you know. But it can wait."

They worked quietly for a while, breaking the silence to comment on the fast melting snow or to share ideas about Christmas gifts for Pops and the boys. Beth told about the songs the school chorus was practicing for the concert. Mom hoped to get to the store on Friday for a special yarn sale.

Just before noon they had both cakes in the oven and three sheets of cookies ready to decorate. Mom suggested they take a break for lunch and watch her regular TV show. As they tuned in, Jack Pierce was giving a special report.

"Hi-de-ho, folks. This is your Precision Predictor Jack-Boy himself. Sorry about all that snow last night. It snuck by me, so to speak. That was nice, fluffy stuff, though. Snow plows had no trouble with it. But I'm here now to tell you I have got ONE SUPER STORM comin' up." Turning to the large map behind him, Jack shifted blue arrows and self-stick clouds around as he spoke.

"This one's comin' from Canada over the Great Lakes. Plenty of wind and wetness. Possible hail and sleet. So, move fast and get where you're goin' for the holidays. Then stay indoors with your family and friends and turkey and plum puddin'. Take care now. Hurry home cautiously. Good luck!" He smiled, saluted, and turned to accept a long red muffler and an umbrella from a pretty female co-worker.

Jack's last words were interrupted by the phone ringing. Bess picked it up and spoke in snatches. "Yes, of course, Joy.... Fine with me.... About one o'clock.... Good." Beth hadn't a clue until her mother hung up and told her Joy's message.

"Joy said that Bud had called her to say he was bringing the children home. The rink manager had his radio on and heard the weather report. He wants to close early and go home himself. Bud said for Joy to find out when Pops planned to leave his office. He wants to pick up Pops in the city and go together to the airport for Dan. Joy suggested the boys play with Susie and Joey in the cellar game room for the afternoon. Then when the others get in, you and I can go over and have supper with them."

"Is she worried about Dan?" asked Beth.

"She didn't say. Early this morning when Bud called about the skating, he told us Dan phoned last night, saying he was getting the earliest flight out today. It had snowed in Kansas last week, but was clear now. I imagine Dan's worst weather will be here. This storm's coming from the north. Canada, wasn't it?"

Beth agreed, "That's right. He's headed into it. Maybe he'll get here first!"

"Let's hope so," said Bess. "How about eating our lunch now and then getting on with preparations for tomorrow's celebrations? We're ahead so far. Maybe we can finish before we go next door."

Mother and daughter ate sandwiches and hot chocolate for lunch, as they watched the "continuing drama" which they had "joined in progress." When they finished, they decided to leave the TV on to keep updated on the weather. Besides, Jack Pierce put on a good show.

Beth, looking out of the window when she heard Bud's van, saw all the children troop into the Benson house. Joy ran out to give Bud a thermos and what was probably his favorite, a cheese steak sandwich, wrapped in aluminum foil. The sky was darkening as he pulled away and Joy turned back.

46

"Aunt Joy is coming here," Beth said, as she went to open the door.

"The whole neighborhood's younger generation is in our cellar, so I can't stay here long," Joy announced. "Just came to tell you Dan phoned. He's landed safely. I called Pops and he's going to wait for Bud and ride with him to get Dan. It will make him later getting home, but he prefers it to traveling on the speed line and bus. Say! You two are cooking up a storm right here! These look delicious!"

"Thank you, Joy. We've had a peaceful morning. With luck we'll be done by suppertime and have only the last-minute things to do tomorrow," smiled Bess.

"Well, with the mob at my house, I'd better get back," sighed Joy. "See you tonight."

An hour later it began to snow, and Bess noticed all the children except her boys leave for their homes. Minutes later Joey knocked and opened their door.

"Susie and the guys are still playing, but I asked Mom if I could come over to visit and maybe help decorate cookies or something. Alright, Aunt Bess?"

"Delighted! We're always glad to see you, dear," Bess assured her. "The cookies are done, but maybe you'd like to draw turkeys or pilgrims for place cards. You know where the paper and paste and other things are." She gestured toward the drawer which held those items. "Switch on the lights while you're over there, please. It got dark all of a sudden."

Both girls exclaimed about the wind and snow that was slanting across the window. Joey flipped the lights on, and began to assemble what she needed for the cards. All three turned to the TV as Jack Pierce appeared in scarf and ear muffs. "Hi-de-ho, folks. He-e-e-er-e she comes! This one's not sneakin' around. She's spittin' and howlin' somethin' fierce. Travelin' fast enough to be gone in a few hours, though…"

There was a crash, a bright flash outdoors, and then Jack's face disappeared as the TV and every other light in the house went out.

Beth screamed as she felt something grab her.

XI

"Don't be frightened, girls. Just stand still," Bess Baker's voice was reassuring. A moment later the beam of the flashlight she held swept the room.

Joey let go. "I'm sorry, Beth, I didn't mean to scare you," she apologized. "The noise and the flash startled me."

"It's alright, honey," laughed Beth. "I bet you're the softest 'monster' that ever grabbed anybody!" With a glance out the window, Beth added, "We seem to be the only house in darkness."

"I'll take a look down the cellar at the fuse box," said Bess as she began to leave the room.

Beth turned toward her, "Wait a minute, Mom. Someone's coming."

The door opened and Dick entered, stamping snow off his boots. "Everybody OK here?" he asked. "We saw the flash and thought we heard a scream...."

"We're alright, but Jack Pierce died," giggled Beth.

"Well, he was dressed to kill," added Joey, "ear muffs and all."

Dick was disgusted. "Honestly, you girls really bug me. I can't remember when I last heard a sensible statement from either of you."

Bess, who'd had to bite her lip to keep from laughing, put her hand on Dick's arm. She admitted to herself that both the frustration of her son and the girls' joking that caused it were funny. "Don't be annoyed, Dick. We were all frightened. Thank you for coming to help us. I was about to check the fuse box in the cellar. Every house on the block has lights but ours. Come with me."

Dick, ignoring the girls, said, "I'll go down by myself, Mom. Aunt Joy says to come over now. When Pops and Bud and Dan get in, they can see what happened. Why don't you all get ready while I go to the cellar?"

They were all bundled warmly when he returned. "Looks like lightning struck our circuit box. That kills all the electricity. No danger of fire, but it will take a while to fix."

"What about food in the refrigerator and freezer?" asked Bess.

"It will stay cold enough if the door's not opened, I think," Dick replied. "Besides, now the heat will go off in the house."

Beth couldn't resist asking, "Lightning in a snow storm?"

"Strange things sometimes happen, dear," her mother answered quickly. Those two really couldn't speak decently to each other. Hoping to head off Dick's reply to Beth, she said, "Well, let's go."

They were amazed to find such extremely unpleasant blizzard-like conditions outside. The new snow was wet and sloppy. Piled on top of last night's, it was more than a foot deep in spots. The wind was strong, and it drove the cold and wet against them with surprising force. Dick supported Joey. Beth and her mother leaned against each other. It took nearly five minutes to go the short distance between the two houses.

Joy was standing inside the door to take their wet coats when they arrived, and the warm glow in the room behind was a wonderful sight. They seemed to have stepped into a completely different world. In fact, they had. Rusty, Tom, and Susie had pulled the sofa over and moved every available chair, small rug, and large pillow around the coffee table which stood in front of the fireplace. Lively flames danced and crackled, adding their own brightness to the smiles of the children.

The feeling of concern for Dan, Bud, and Pops was still present, but the safe arrival of the four who had just entered seemed a good omen. True, they had come only from next door, yet they doubled the number in this cozy room.

"When Bud and Dan were building this fireplace last August," said Joy, "I pictured a scene like this in my mind."

Tom smiled, "I remember what Bud said then. 'In February, when the clock said noon and the thermometer showed ten below, I knew how I'd spend August.'"

Joey, who'd been frightened in the dark Baker home and wind-tossed in the storm outside, moved gratefully into the warm circle of the fire's glow. She stood facing the fire with arms stretched wide. While everyone waited, almost expecting a prayer or other serious utterance, she declared, "We're gonna have a SUPER Christmas!"

Susie laughed, "We haven't even had Thanksgiving yet!"

"Sure," answered Joey, not in the least deflated, "but it's all holiday time now. Besides, we'll be next door for most of tomorrow."

Bess turned to Joy. "Has Dan seen the fireplace lit, yet?" she asked. "Seems to me he left before the colder weather set in."

"You're right," her friend replied. "Dan's been away eight or nine weeks. It was too warm before he left. He'll really appreciate it today, I imagine."

49

"It can't miss," Dick assured them. "Just coming across the yard has helped me understand how travelers in times past looked forward to a fire. How the thought of it could keep them going. And how comforting it must have been to arrive at an inn or a friend's house and be shown to a seat by the fireplace." He was so sincere that no one, especially Beth, even considered teasing about this uncharacteristically poetic speech. Actually, this was the sort of thing she'd thought Joey was going to say.

"Speaking of travelers, here come our very own three." This was from Rusty, who had appointed himself lookout, and was standing at the window.

Joy and Bess hurried to the door, and the children all followed quickly. There was much happy noise and confusion as the family tried to welcome their "very own travelers" without getting wet themselves, and the three men tried to shed their own soaked coats and boots without also brushing off the loving hugs and kisses.

As soon as she had greeted Pops and made sure he was safe, Bess went to the kitchen for the hot coffee Joy had prepared. She carried the pot and fixin's to the fireplace, leaving Joy free to enjoy her son's return.

Beth hung back slightly to give the others a chance to greet Dan first. As she watched them, she felt again the magic of Dan's presence and the special quality he possessed. He managed to convey great warmth and love to his own family, without letting the Bakers feel in any way slighted. His dark hair waved handsomely above clear hazel eyes, and his broad smile was genuine. He exchanged with the boys their Secret Feline Friendclasp, and gathered the girls together in a giant bear hug.

When they were finally all seated around the kitchen table enjoying the supper of spaghetti, meat balls, garlic bread, and salad that Joy and Susie had prepared, Dan gave an account of his trip. "The flight was the easiest part," he began. Beth and her mother exchanged glances, for this was what they'd told each other earlier. "I'd just turned from the baggage pick-up when I saw Bud and Pops," Dan continued. "Then the fun began. I guess every traveler had at least two people at the airport who had heard the bad weather report and come to pick him up. The traffic was really more hazardous than the storm at that point. We were lucky, though. The wind didn't start in earnest until we'd crossed the bridge. Then it was Dad who had to deal with the difficult driving." He turned to his father by way of passing the story to him.

Bud obliged, "Well, I was glad we had the van rather than the car. It's heavier and is built higher. We had some tools in the back, and Dan's luggage to add ballast. We also had Pops, here." He looked kindly at his neighbor, while everyone laughed at the thought that the slight, five-foot-three accountant would help weigh anything down.

Pops didn't mind jokes about his size. He'd long ago learned, when challenged, to quote his father, "It's the brains that count, not how high you carry them." He'd proved it time and again, too. Also, Pops knew that Bud wanted his company this day, as he often did, not for the bulk he brought to the project. He had been the one to remind Bud that Ashwood was always slow to plow their streets. A route through Lakeside might be greater in distance, but would be safer and take less time in the long run.

This was just what Bud was telling everyone now, "So, we didn't have to deal with unplowed roads at all," he concluded. "But let's consider going over to see exactly what caused the trouble next door, my friends."

"Right now?" Dick asked. "It's so terribly miserable out, and since we know the circuit box was hit…"

"I'm sure you're right about what shut down the lights, Dick," answered Pops, "but I'd feel better if I knew there was no other damage. Also, if the heat's gone off, we can't sleep there tonight. Maybe it can be fixed easily. If not, the sooner we determine that the better, too.

"If you and Dan will hold the fort here, Tom and Rusty can take their turns braving the storm and come with Bud and me. Alright with the rest of you?"

It was decided as Pops had suggested, and soon four pairs of feet were stamping snow onto Bess Baker's small vestibule rug. Bud and Tom went to the cellar. Pops and Rusty began a room to room check of the house. They disconnected all electrical equipment, from freezer and TV to alarm clocks. They also stuffed newspapers around all windows facing north and west. The house seemed to get colder even as they worked. No really serious problems were found.

In half an hour the converging of flashlights in the kitchen indicated the inspection of the house had been completed. Bud reported there was no immediate danger, so no need to try making

51

repairs at night. He suggested all return to the Benson home and begin celebrating Thanksgiving by spending the night there, together. The mothers could organize sleeping arrangements.

Pops agreed, and the boys were delighted.

XII

While the girls cleaned up in the kitchen, and Joy and Bess fluffed pillows and emptied ashtrays by the fire, Dan and Dick went to the cellar for more logs. On an impulse, Dick decided to try telling Dan about the things that had been bothering him. Even as the thought was forming in his mind, Dan gave him an opening.

"So, pal, what's new and interesting in your life? I hear regularly from our females, in fact Joey's become quite a letter writer. But aside from that Masked Lion card at Hallowe'en, I've heard nothing from you."

"Oh, lots of action. The football and school stuff's the same as usual. But I get thoughts and feelings I've never had before—and I get kinda scared. I don't understand some of it. Sure, it's great being the biggest kids in Elm Street School, but it's our last year there. That makes it kinda sad. Those mixed, happy and sad feelings I can understand. What upsets me is other stuff. Makes me want to fight and yell." Dick had been talking to Dan's back as they descended the stairs.

Now, at the bottom, Dan turned to face the young boy, and spoke sympathetically, "I know about wanting to fight and yell when things don't make sense. What sort of things aren't making sense to you?"

"Mainly Beth and her spooky ideas about that trunk. But they wouldn't be so spooky all by themselves. You know everyone says I'm scientific minded. Well, if that means I like to know why things happen and what to expect, they're right," Dick was finding it easier to express himself now. "Well, our first unit in Science this fall was on sound. Mr. Len had us each make a project. I did a wooden xylophone. It was really good, and the kids were interested in seeing how the loosely nailed pieces of wood of different sizes would vibrate in different tones. It was a new idea to them, but easy to understand."

Dick, quite comfortable with his story now, added, "It was sorta—having a thing your mind could touch and hold."

Dan encouraged him, "OK. I follow. Where's the problem?"

"So, Benny brought in his slide trombone," Dick continued, "and he borrowed a snare drum from the music room. He set up the drum next to Mr. Len's desk. Then he went to the back of the room and blew his horn... AND THE DRUM VIBRATED!" Dick's eyes got bigger, and he seemed frightened even then. "Ben blew different notes and the drum vibrated for a longer time!"

Dan spoke seriously, not laughing at Dick, "Surely you've heard of 'being on the same wave length' or 'picking up a friendly vibration?'"

"Yea, I've HEARD of it, but it never really happened, I thought...." Dick was suddenly concerned that the others would wonder where they were. He began walking toward the wood pile, but kept on talking. "That was just the beginning. The drum didn't act the way I'd expected, but then people began acting funny, too."

"People?"

"Rusty doesn't hang around with us as much as he used to. He wanders off sketching trees and stuff. Then Beth says she 'feels' there's something in an old, dumb trunk. I even had trouble beating Joey in a race at the rink today! What really did it was the lightning out of the snow storm."

Dan did laugh at that speech, "You do indeed have a lot to think about," he admitted. He stooped to pick up a log. "Here, have some. Rusty and Joey are just growing up; and Beth does seem to be on the trail of something, from what I hear. I will grant you that lightning in a snow storm is unusual. It's not a people-problem, though."

Dick stood with arms outstretched as Dan stacked them with logs. "Come to think of it," Dick mused, "that lightning may have been good for me. It sent me into the storm, and when I got back I had more appreciation for warm fires and families and good food." Then he smiled, "Seems like the vibrations are attacking me, now."

"It's possible," replied Dan, straightening, with his arms full. "Maybe you'll consider being nicer to Beth?"

Dick considered. "Well, not nicer. Just not as mean. But I do feel better, Dan. Thanks for listenin'," he said, heading for the stairs.

"Anytime."

As the two unloaded their arms at the fireplace, they heard voices in the kitchen. They stacked the logs neatly and joined the group in time to hear that the Bakers would not be able to sleep in their cold house, and would be spending the night.

"Beth can double up with Susie. The boys and Dan can unroll sleeping bags by the fire," Joy was saying. "Bess and Pops should be alright in Dan's room. I'm sure we can find clean pajamas for everyone."

Dick smiled to himself. It looked as if he'd be spending the night by the friendly fire. Right now, though, he was going with his brothers to the Bakers' attic and help Dan get sleeping bags. They hadn't expected to need sleeping bags until summer came and they went on camping trips.

Beth went upstairs with Susie and Joey. The girls would shower now to lighten the bathroom traffic. Then they'd dress in warm robes and slippers and join the others downstairs. They hoped to toast marshmallows. "If there's any left from this afternoon," added Joey.

While Bud replenished the fire and Joy went to check on clean towels, Pops went to the closet to get from his overcoat pocket the marshmallows he'd taken from his own kitchen. When they'd decided to secure the house and spend the night with Bud and Joy, he'd slipped them in his pocket as a surprise.

The adults had just settled comfortably when Dan and the boys appeared with the sleeping bags. These they put in a far corner of the room until needed, and joined their parents around the fire. Tom was carrying something.

"What do you have there, Tom?" his mother asked.

"Something I thought had been thrown out," Tom replied, opening what proved to be the board from an old game of Monopoly.

"Why, I did throw that away nearly a year ago," Bess said.

Joy asked, "May I have a closer look?"

Tom, carrying it to her, explained, "When Pops bought the family a new Monopoly set last Christmas, I pulled the old one from the trash. Rusty, Dick, and I were going to change the names to those of people and places in Shady Oaks and play it ourselves in our room upstairs.

"We started, and Beth said she and Susie would like to help.

54

I guess she brought it here, and after it hung around a while, it got mixed up with stuff here."

Joy laughed. "I do remember it in the girls' room. Then after a while it disappeared."

"The idea of changing the names is good," Pops declared, "but you just pasted labels over the regular names, and they're torn and faded now. Why not get a fresh start?"

"Fresh start at what, Pops?" Beth came in with Susie and Joey. Then, when she saw the board, "Oh, I've often wondered what happened to that! We never found time to finish it...."

Susie spoke up, "We have plenty of time now. But let's really start fresh with a whole new board. Joey, could we use the back of the poster you made last month for Fire Prevention?"

"Sure," answered the youngest girl. "I'll get it, and bring down pencils and rulers and colored markers, too."

Bud spoke up, "One of the best ideas I've heard all day. May I suggest all six of you work on it? There's room for everyone at the kitchen table. You can use the old board to copy measurements for borders and spaces. Be sure to name at least one railroad after me. In the meantime, we parents can visit with Dan."

"And later," added Joy, "we can all roast marshmallows together, thanks to Pops."

The children moved into the kitchen, and Dan sat cross-legged on the floor with his back to the fire. As he looked at the faces encircling him, glowing in the firelight with pride and hope, Dan thought that this must be a classic scene. Down through the ages, the eldest son, returning from an initial venture into the world, would be the center of attention.

And so, this first of the newest Baker-Benson generation, with the voices of the younger ones as a background in the next room, told about his months away from home.

Dan told about the trivial problems of locating classrooms and about the fun of making new friends. He told of the flat, flat land of Kansas. He told of the inspiring lectures of the professor who was convinced his students would one day be designing bridges on the moon. And he reminded them of the monotony of term papers.

This was the day they'd been anticipating, and he did not disappoint them. But Daniel Robert Benson, with the friendly flames warming his back, chose not to mention pretty Peggy Jensen. Peggy's smile warmed his heart, her hair was as soft as corn silk, and her clear brown eyes had had no cause to fill with tears when he left. She knew he'd be back. Someday he'd bring her to sit within this cozy circle with him. But not yet. And she knew that, too.

"Hey, Rusty, that's super! Look, Mom, the cop on the corner here is Police Chief Miller!" Joey called from the kitchen

Joy and Bess, coming out for marshmallows and snacks, bent over the board the children were drawing. "Joey, dear," her mother began, "everything is SUPER to you these days. But, look, Bess, this does resemble Chief Miller!"

"And there's Bud's van in the opposite corner, in the Free Parking Zone!" laughed Bess.

That brought the men out. Pops found each of the Community Chest trunks with the name plate: "Thomas Baker, 1882." Dan's Electric Company was illuminated by a lighted bulb. The Bud Benson RR Company had a Thomas Division, a Dick Division, and a Rusty Division.

Joy's Jewelry Store was where the luxury tax was collected. Just down the street was Bess's Craft Corner, Susie's Sweete Shoppe, and Beth's Boutique. Joey's Parklane Apartments surprised everyone.

"I didn't know you were interested in real estate, Joey," said Bud.

"I'm not, it's just to have something until the toy store is built," the owner explained in a matter of fact tone.

"Why not clear off now? You don't have to take everything all the way upstairs," said Joy, "but put the pencils and markers in their boxes, and just generally give us space here on the table."

Trays of food gradually replaced the children's clutter on the kitchen table, then were transported to the next room. There all the members of both families draped themselves on chairs, pillows, and rugs. They did have the marshmallows, and even sang a few songs. However, they were all more tired than they realized. Nearly everyone had fought the storm at some time during the day. So, when Bess noticed Joey begin to nod, and Beth and Susie to swallow yawns, she nudged Joy. Both mothers stood and began to gather dirty dishes and mugs.

The evening was declared a success. The sleepy girls were followed upstairs by the adults, and the indoor campers were left to make their own arrangements.

Even the wind quieted down, and the world rested. And Jack

Pierce, alive and well in homes throughout town, assured them of sunshine for tomorrow.

XIII

The sun shone all day on Thanksgiving, and the ice and snow began to melt. Traveling up and down the streets of town, the Shady Oaks snow plow cleaned off the main roads, but blocked the driveways of private homes as it passed. It also effectively trapped all cars parked along its route.

After cleaning their own yards, the boys spent the morning earning extra money shoveling sidewalks, unblocking driveways, and freeing parked cars in the neighborhood. Bud and Dan restored the Bakers' electricity, and the original plans for the dinner were carried out.

The two families made it quite a formal occasion. Everyone dressed in Sunday best clothes, and were deeply grateful for the blessings of health, friendship, and all the material goods they possessed.

On Friday, Dan contacted his crowd in town and made the rounds of the skating rink, bowling alley, and Ski Mountain. The younger children finished their Shady Oaks Monopoly board. Joey got her toy shop and gave Tom the apartments. Then they spent the day indoors, playing the game.

Dan was to leave at about noon on Sunday, so the families planned to spend Saturday evening together. They had at first thought of gathering around the Bensons' fireplace again. However, on Saturday morning Joey suggested putting on a play for Dan, telling the story of Belle and Tom. They could use the clothes from the trunk, couldn't they? And the Baker house? The stairs would make a grand entrance scene.

Bess was at first reluctant. It seemed to be encouraging the importance Beth gave to the trunk and its contents. Pops, however, pointed out that the style of the old clothes made them impractical for everyday wear, while their good quality gave them a chance to survive being used as costumes. "Besides," he added, "Tom and Belle, if they could know, would probably like to be remembered by the present generation of young people. I'd be flattered if the twenty-first-century Bakers found me interesting enough to impersonate."

"Well, alright. This is a good holiday for recalling our ancestors. Maybe they'll get tired of it all after this."

So, Joey, Beth, and Susie settled down on Saturday morning to write a script. They agreed that Joey could be Belle.

"I do wish I could find a red wig somewhere," she declared. "I know we're not sure if Belle had red hair, but we're not sure she didn't either. That gives us a fifty-fifty chance."

Tom, overhearing her, shook his head, "The way girls think," he told himself, "I'll never understand 'em. What about black, brown, or blonde hair?"

But Joey was working on something else already. "You can be Edna, Susie, since you like her so well," the young playwright declared. "Suppose we open with you writing the letter? You can read it as you write, and it will be a super-real way to begin the whole play."

Susie smiled, "Alright," she agreed.

"And, Beth, I'd love you for a sister. We know so little about Belle, we could give her one. What do you think?" Joey asked.

"Why not her best friend?" suggested Beth. "I'm your friend, now. The part will be easy to act. We could make Dick the lawyer that Tom worked for, and Rusty can be Dick's son. He can become Tom's best friend...."

"And Rusty can be Beth's beau," continued Susie.

Both girls let Joey complete the plot, and they weren't disappointed. "And Rusty will introduce Tom to Belle! It COULD have happened...!" Joey was delighted.

Susie got the original letter from Aunt Bess and made a copy, returning the precious heirloom as soon as possible. Then she practiced reading it several times. She could almost picture the kind, gentle Edna, and she wanted very much to convey to Dan and the others the goodness of this simple mountain woman.

Meanwhile, Beth and Joey had been literally putting words into the mouths of the lawyer, his son, Belle, and Tom. When Susie joined them again, they were discussing how to arrange a nineteenth-century version of a double date. "Tom should bring her a gift, don't you think? Maybe a box of candy," Joey was saying.

Beth laughed. "And you figure we can have Tom actually give you some candy!"

Joey laughed, too. "Well, why not? I'll share it with you."

Susie joined in, "Then the next time, you can present him with some homemade cookies to munch while he studies the law books."

The boys had agreed to practice after lunch, so all six children gathered downstairs to stage their performance. The girls had written each part a second time on a separate paper, so each could have his own copy. After her opening scene, Susie didn't appear "on stage" again, but acted as director and prompter.

Dick, having recently allowed himself to consider vibrations, found he could also enjoy make-believe and even once-upon-a-time. He had barely tolerated dressing up when the trunk was first opened. Now he entered into the spirit of the play, and suggested an added touch.

"Why not bring down some of the books as well as the costumes? We can use them as props in my office."

That evening Dan and the four parents were, of course, prepared to enjoy whatever the children presented. However, Susie's reading of Edna's letter was so sincere that the sight of Dick rising from behind a desk piled high with leather bound books was a logical scene. Dick's kindly greeting to his new apprentice, Tom, dressed in a slightly too large homespun suit, followed naturally, also.

The now delighted audience wasn't at all surprised at the instant friendship between the lawyer's son, Rusty, and the new apprentice. They were equally prepared to hear Rusty suggest the double date, and to find Tom reluctant to agree.

"How can I hope to find favor with such a grand lady?" Tom asked, with a sad glance at his homespun.

"Although I do not know her well," Rusty replied, "if Miss Isabelle Jefferson is a good friend of my beloved Beth, she is surely a kind lady."

Tom allowed himself to be persuaded, and everyone waited for the next scene, while the books were gathered up and comfortable chairs were brought to replace the straight ones that had furnished the "law office."

Dan and Bud did some volunteer work as stagehands. They were glad to help, but even more anxious to hasten the showing of a performance they were willing to admit was very interesting. Pops sat back quietly, preferring to help by not getting in the way of people who knew what they were doing.

"I'm anxious to see what Joey did with her hair," whispered

Joy to Bess. "I overheard her trying to talk Susie into helping her color it with Clairol. I trusted Susie's good sense even before I heard her say there was a better way."

In the kitchen, Dick was proposing a change in script to Rusty. "They have Tom giving Joey candy and you handing Beth flowers, don't they, Rusty?" he asked.

"Yea," Rusty laughed, "then we'll all get to eat the candy. Those girls are somethin'."

"OK on the candy," said Dick, "if you can eat and talk at the same time. I'm sure they can! But I'd like to try a surprise. When I went for the books today, I found this one. How about giving it to Beth as your present to her? Make up something clever about the title." He handed Rusty a very beautifully bound leather volume. It might have been a diary, as it had a clasp. There was a title embossed on the spine, though. A most unusual item. Rusty read the title, and looked up in surprise.

"How did we miss this before?"

"I pretty much rushed things when we emptied the trunk, remember?"

Rusty nodded. "This could surprise a lot of us. It's shaped like a book, but doesn't feel like a book, exactly. The clasp isn't locked. Did you open it?"

Dick evaded answering by pointing out, "They're ready for the next scene, I think."

XIV

No one was ready for the Isabelle Jefferson who now descended the stairs with her best friend! Her long blue dress trailing gracefully, the heroine fanned her glowing cheeks and smiled sweetly. Joey knew that pinning her hair up, and powdering it, was just the touch needed to make her the Belle she wanted to be. And the spontaneous applause from her audience confirmed this knowledge.

The children continued smoothly in their lines, until Rusty handed Beth the gift package he'd brought. She was expecting the half-dozen plastic roses they'd wrapped and tied this afternoon. Instead, her brother was handing her a book, and making an original speech.

"Last week, on my trip to Philadelphia, I chanced to see this in the window of Ye Olde Booke Shoppe on Broad Street. Remarking the title, and knowing your interest in romantic novels, I dared to hope you would be pleased if I purchased it for you." Rusty extended the book.

Beth took it, and slowly turned it to read the title. "It's called *Lady Elizabeth's Gift*," she said. "But there's no author or publisher named." She'd stopped being Belle Jefferson's friend and become Beth Baker, lover of romantic novels.

Belle, too, became Joey Benson, Curious Person Number One, as she cried, "Open it, Beth!"

Beth flipped the clasp and exclaimed, "It's not a book at all!" While everyone watched, she lifted from the book-shaped box an oilskin packet. She handed the box to Rusty and then sat on the nearest chair to unfold the packet in her lap. The play was forgotten as everyone gathered around the young girl.

Beth drew from the oilskin a red velvet jewelry box. She carefully lifted the lid and held up, for all to see, a diamond necklace. The sudden discovery of such pure beauty stunned them all. They watched in silence as the lights flashed and the perfect stones, hanging from Beth's trembling fingers, swung slowly back and forth.

It was Dick who spoke first, "Behold, the treasure in our attic. Looks like the vibrations were right after all."

"What do you know about this, son?" Pops turned to Dick.

Dick then explained his idea to use the books as props in the play. When he went up to the attic for them, he chose the pile he and Susie had removed so quickly from the trunk several weeks before. As he stacked them in a carton to carry them down, he noticed this particular one. He saved it out and suggested to Rusty to surprise Beth with it during the play. Well, yes, he had flipped the lid and found the packet, but hadn't opened it. He'd figured Beth could have the pleasure of that.

"Is there no clue about where it came from?" asked Bud.

Beth turned the red velvet box over and over. Then she began to spread the oilskin flat. Folded inside one edge was a parchment-like paper.

"There's only a few words I can make out," Beth told them. "Here's 'To Brave Captain Jeremy Baker... saving life... infant son...' Pops, you try."

Her father took the parchment. He turned it toward the light much as he'd turned Edna's letter when he'd first tried to read that. It seemed a kind of ritual. "That looks to be about all that's left. No, near the end, 'protecting...these diamonds...my gratitude forever.' Ah, here's a name, too. 'Lady Elizabeth S...' the rest is too faded, " he sighed.

"What's really missing is something by Grandfather Baker to tie this all together," declared Bess.

Dan spoke up, "Let's see the book-shaped box, Rusty," he asked. Then, when holding it, "A classmate of mine in Kansas described something like this an ancestor of his packed in his covered wagon. Came from the Blue Ridge Mountains in Virginia, he told us. We thought he was making it up." Dan turned the box over. "There's supposed to be a hidden spring.... There!"

The bottom of the box, formed as the back cover of the book, swung free. A paper fell out.

"You know," said Susie, to no one in particular, "if I read all this in a story somewhere, I wouldn't believe a single word of it."

"Here you go, Pops," said Dan, handing the head of the Baker Clan the latest piece of family history.

Once more everyone's attention was focused on Pops, and this time he read the most unique message of all:

To my Beloved Wife,

It is my will that you not receive this until my death. I have so directed my lawyers, and I trust they will do as I wish.

There is a legend in the Baker family that a brave sea captain once saved the life of an English lady and her only son, an infant. In gratitude, she gave him a diamond necklace. The diamonds were real and of truly great value. But of even more value was the good fortune they brought. As long as the owner treated his family and friends lovingly and justly, he would never suffer extreme material or spiritual poverty.

Thomas McCloskey, my foster father, who was also my mother's cousin, told me this when I left his care. He and his wife, Edna, passed the diamonds on to me. They belong to the oldest Baker, male or female.

I'm adding to the gift for you. I've had a mountain craftsman make a clever box, shaped like a book. He could not pay me the legal fee he owed for my services, and I could not find anyone else to make you so unique a gift.

62

So, we called it a fair exchange.

Thank you, dearest Belle, for your love and for our life together. I'll be waiting for you.

Tom

"Well, Princess, it seems that your 'vibrations,' as Dick calls them, were right all along. I think your mother will agree that the box may be yours right now. It pretty much has your name on it, in fact! However, the jewels and the letters would be best in our safe deposit box at the bank." Pops knew Bess was nodding agreement even before he looked at her.

Beth smiled delightedly as she handed the necklace to her father, and received the box in exchange. Dan moved over to show her how to operate the spring release on the bottom, and Joey leaned against her for a closer look. Tom winked at Susie. Dick and Rusty shook hands.

The rest of the evening was spent discussing the many interesting things that had happened to both families since the Feline Defenders of the Future had pushed an old trunk from under the eaves.

As she pulled the covers to her chin that night, Beth smiled to herself. The gypsy had been right all along, too. The stars and the cups of the cards meant diamonds and love, Madame had told her. Not only had there been a treasure of diamonds in their attic, but finding them had been an adventure which strengthened the ties of love and kindness among family and friends.

And now Beth had her own special treasure box, *Lady Elizabeth's Gift*. It had been ordered, made, and owned by long ago people who probably never dreamed there'd be an Elizabeth Rachel Baker of Silver Maple Land in Shady Oaks, New Jersey...Earth...Universe.